BOUDICA:
THE SECRETS OF THE DRUIDS

CAROLINE CORBY was born and brought up in London. She studied mathematics and statistics at Bristol University, then became a banker and spent thirteen years in the City, ending up as a director in a venture capital company before deciding to leave her job to spend more time with her young family.

Caroline has always enjoyed history and wanted to find a historical novel aimed at children that would capture her daughter's imagination. After searching without success, she decided to write one herself and the Before They Were Famous series was born. It explores the early lives of some of history's most fascinating characters, who, in shifting, dangerous worlds, struggle to make their mark and become heroes of the future. Of *Boudica: The Secrets of the Druids*, Caroline says: "I've always been intrigued by Boudica, a warrior queen who defied the might of the Roman Empire."

Caroline lives in Hampstead, North London, with her husband and three daughters aged fourteen, twelve and ten.

Other titles in the series

Cleopatra: Escape Down the Nile

Upcoming titles

William the Conqueror: Nowhere to Hide

Pocahontas: A Princess Betrayed

Lady Jane Grey: A Queen for Sale

Julius Caesar: The Boy that Conquered the World

CAROLINE CORBY

BOUDICA

THE SECRETS OF THE DRUIDS

WALKER
BOOKS

This is a work of fiction. Names, characters, places and incidents
are either the product of the author's imagination or, if real, are used fictitiously.
All statements, activities, stunts, descriptions, information and material of any other
kind contained herein are included for entertainment purposes only and should
not be relied on for accuracy or replicated as they may result in injury.

First published 2008 by Walker Books Ltd
87 Vauxhall Walk, London SE11 5HJ

2 4 6 8 10 9 7 5 3 1

Text © 2008 Caroline Corby

The right of Caroline Corby to be identified as author of this work has been asserted
by her in accordance with the Copyright, Designs and Patents Act 1988

This book has been typeset in Usherwood and Herculanum

Printed in Great Britain by Clays Ltd, St Ives plc

British Library Cataloguing in Publication Data:
a catalogue record for this book is available from the British Library

ISBN: 978-1-4063-1253-9

www.walkerbooks.co.uk

For Grace

SPRING, AD 43

"HOW long to go now?"

"Boudica, I told you not to ask me again," said a stout woman, stirring a pot of stew. An older woman was stripping meat from a bone. All three were huddled close to a fire, their cheeks glowing in the heat.

"Please, Hendra. Just tell me when you think they'll come?"

The heavy woman put down her spoon.

"Let me see. Last night they'll have camped at Bodras. We're a good day's ride away, so I reckon the earliest you can expect them is when the sun touches the tip of the forest. That's if they make good time. What do you think, Argent?"

"Sounds about right to me."

The girl jumped up, ran to the far side of the wattle house, and pulled back a fur covering a doorway. A blast of icy air sent smoke from the fire whirling. Boudica looked across the valley to the wood, her red hair billowing in the bitterly cold draught.

"That's not long; I need to go."

She stepped out into the misty afternoon light.

"Boudica, come back. You've got to help. There's a feast to get ready."

The girl reappeared.

"I will. I've just got to get something for my father. It's his present. It must be ready when he comes."

"You haven't even got a fur on. You'll freeze," called Hendra, but there was no response.

"She's wild, that one," complained Argent, pushing a strand of grey hair out of her eyes. Her gnarled fingers glistened with fat from the meat. "I won't be sorry when she leaves the tribe. You never know what she's up to."

"She's wild all right," said Hendra, "but I'll miss her. She's the bravest girl I've ever known. You've seen the way she rides a horse: none of the boys can touch her. Anyway she hasn't seen her family for over a year. You can't blame her for being excited."

The door creaked open and a tall woman with frizzy, black hair entered. She was wearing a blue tartan dress pinned with a brooch and a thick torc, a heavy band of twisted gold, round her neck.

Hendra nudged Argent and said under her breath, "Watch out, Queen Cartimandua's here."

Both women hastily got to their feet.

"Where's Boudica?" demanded the queen.

"She's gone out, ma'am. I'm sure she'll be back soon."

Queen Cartimandua pursed her lips.

"Hendra, that girl is supposed to be in your care, but you never seem to know where she is."

"Sorry, ma'am."

"I want to see her. She must look respectable when her parents turn up, otherwise they'll wonder what we've been doing with her. Do you understand?"

"Yes, ma'am. I'll go and find her straightaway."

Hendra had a shrewd idea that Boudica would be with Culann, the town blacksmith. The two were as thick as thieves. She tried to picture Boudica when she'd left. As usual her hair was tangled, there was almost certainly mud on her skirt and her hem was bound to be ripped. Somehow it always was. And that was before she went to Culann's. She'd be even grubbier when she got back. Hendra sighed. It was impossible to keep Boudica from looking scruffy.

Boudica felt like jumping for joy as she ran through the town. She was going to be reunited with her family. She hadn't seen them since last spring when she'd left her tribe, the Iceni, to journey northwards. Aged eleven, the children of the royal household and of the king's most senior warriors were expected to spend a year with another tribe. Jodoc, Boudica's father, was principal counsellor to Antedios, King of the Iceni, and so Boudica had been sent away to the Brigantes. Relations between this tribe and the Iceni had been difficult ever since Queen Cartimandua inherited the Brigantian throne. The Iceni hoped an exchange would improve things. Now Boudica had done her bit and would soon be heading home.

She arrived at a wattle building. It was smaller than the other houses in Canna, the largest Brigantian town, and was set apart. Despite the perishing wind, the door was open. A wiry hunting dog trotted out and barked half-heartedly.

"Mutta, don't be silly, it's me," said Boudica, patting the dog's head. "Those puppies are making you such a worrier."

She gave the dog a reassuring stroke and went inside, where the singeing heat of a furnace dominated a room crowded with a jumble of dusty mallets, ingots, and piles of charcoal. In the far corner was a wicker basket with three tiny puppies in it. They were so young they looked like grey balls of fur. Mutta settled down to feed her litter.

A lanky boy of thirteen stood next to the hearth, delicately knocking a ball of clay with a hammer. The boy's hair was streaked with soot but that did little to diminish its amazing colour – a vivid ginger, not auburn or red-tinged, but bright orange, like a piece of rusted iron. On top of gangly legs and arms that had yet to fill out, this wiry, luminescent mop announced to even the most casual of observers that the boy was not from these parts. The Brigantes were dark, bronzed, and stocky, everything that Culann was not. Boudica had noticed him as soon as she arrived in Canna and had decided then and there that they would be friends. After all, the two flame-haired children could have been brother and sister. It had taken persistence, as Culann was a natural loner, but her determination had paid off. He was the only person in the town she would miss.

"Hello," called Boudica.

Culann turned round, his smutty, freckled face full of concentration. "Stay there," he ordered.

Despite this instruction, Boudica tiptoed over. She watched quietly as Culann tapped the terracotta sphere, skilfully chipping away chunks of clay. A sliver of bronze appeared. It grew and grew, and a tiny dagger, adorned with fine red and blue lines that twisted like the wind, emerged before her eyes.

"It's lovely!" Boudica couldn't help exclaiming. "It's just what I wanted."

Culann turned round, exasperated.

"I thought I told you to stand back," he said, pushing an unruly curl out of his eye.

"I'm sorry. Have I ruined the surprise?"

Culann rolled his eyes and smiled.

"I suppose not, as it's not really for you."

He handed her the miniature dagger and she examined it carefully. It looked like a toy, but the glinting blade was sharp. The metal handle was carved with the swirling lines that she had come to associate so strongly with the Brigantes. It was traditional for a returning child to give a gift to their father, and this would be perfect.

"Culann, thank you so much. My father will love it,"

she said at last.

Just then a horse thundered past, its rider shouting, "They're coming into the valley. The Iceni are here."

Boudica looked across at the wood. The sun was still way above the tips of the trees. Her parents had made much better time than Hendra had forecast. Suddenly she was gripped with excitement.

"I've got to go. I'll see you at the feast tonight."

"Where are you off to in such a hurry?"

"I'm going to meet my parents and ride with them into the town."

"Boudica, don't. The queen won't want you to and you're covered in soot," Culann called after her but she was gone.

Moments later Hendra came in, panting.

"Where's Boudica?" she asked. "I thought she'd be with you."

"She was. You just missed her. She's gone to meet the Iceni."

"Oh no." Hendra looked horrified. "Couldn't you stop her?"

Culann smiled. "What do you think?"

"Well, I only hope the prince who's replacing her will be less trouble," said Hendra, shaking her head. "He can't be any more."

2

BOUDICA ran straight from Culann's forge to the pasture where the Brigantes' finest horses were kept. Over twenty were grazing quietly in a field. As she untied her favourite and led her out of the paddock, a twinge of guilt ran through her. This was not her horse. She was still too young to have one of her own and so far she had always asked Probas, the brusque man in charge of the herd, before she borrowed one. *But I don't have time now*, she told herself. *Probas could be anywhere. By the time I find him, my parents will be here.*

Deftly she grabbed the mane of the sleek reddish-brown bay, pulled her woollen skirt to her knees and jerked herself up. On the mare's forehead was the odd splash of white, shaped like three overlapping circles, which had given her her name.

"Come on, Clover," Boudica whispered excitedly as she spurred the horse's flank. "Let's meet them at the ridge."

Clover seemed to understand her urgency. She flattened her ears and sprang forward. Boudica grabbed her powerful neck just in time as they hurtled into the forest. In moments they were clear of the trees and on higher, open ground, speeding up towards the top of the hill where the Iceni must appear at any moment. The earth rushed past as Clover's hooves pounded the ground. Boudica's grey shawl flapped around her shoulders and the horse's black mane flicked her face, making her cheeks sting, but she did nothing to slow the pace down.

The hill grew steeper. Clover was snorting great clouds of steam and there was lather on her neck but she galloped on. *If only I had an animal like this*, Boudica thought. From the age of four she'd been given riding lessons by her father and by eight she rode better than many of the older boys. When she was ten, her father had set her a challenge – to master his horse, Kelpa. Kelpa was one of the finest stallions in the Iceni herd, tall and haughty with a sleek, black hide. To begin with he had been skittish, but Boudica was determined. She knew that if she could ride Kelpa, she could ride anything. Day after day she'd persevered, falling several times in the process, but gradually she'd earned his trust. Together they would fly across the Iceni fields in the early morning mist before Boudica's mother, Dagma, called her to her chores.

Before she'd left for Canna, Boudica had pleaded with her father for a horse of her own, after all she was from the Iceni – the tribe of the horse – but so far he had refused. She needed to earn an animal and she could only do so by bringing honour to the tribe. He would reconsider after her stay with the Brigantes.

What better way to show that I'm ready, thought Boudica, *than by greeting him at full pelt?*

Clover raced on up the steep valley. It was the kind of ride Boudica loved, fast and furious. She and Culann often raced each other across the moors. Hendra had once joked that with their flaming, red hair billowing behind them they could be mistaken for a couple of Caledonian marauders, roaring down from the wild north. The joke was tactless; Culann had immediately retreated into silence. He always did whenever the subject of his mysterious parentage came up. Boudica had asked Hendra about it later.

"He was found in a wood a few miles from here, when he was only a child of two or three, wandering alone with no food and only a blanket round his little shoulders. He'd been left behind by his clansmen who must have been up to no good or they wouldn't have run off so quickly. It must have broken his mother's heart. Still he ended up here, so things didn't turn out so badly. Can you imagine if we hadn't taken him in? Even if he'd survived, he'd have been tribe-less, with nowhere to call home."

Except, thought Boudica as she rode up the crag, Culann wasn't ever really at home in Canna. He was always the outsider. He didn't know who he was or where he came from and she knew it bothered him more than he would ever say. Blood and tribe were everything and he wasn't a true Brigantian. Next year, at the age of fourteen, he should become a warrior but, unlike the other boys in the town, he wasn't being trained. He never attended sword and chariot lessons. Nobody told him not to but nobody ever invited him. Boudica, the only other outsider in Canna, was his only friend.

Suddenly, she spotted a group of people on horses at the top of the hill. It must be the Iceni, she thought, digging her heels into Clover's flank.

She felt the mare try to go faster. Her parents were now less than half a mile away. For some reason, she wasn't sure why, she was determined to meet them at the summit.

The ground became even steeper. There were no trees or hedges, only moorland scattered with rocks, stones and the occasional sheep. The terrain was dangerously uneven but Clover picked her way beautifully through the boulders. A man was pointing in their direction. Boudica spurred the horse one last time and then, when she was only a couple of hundred yards away, she felt something give. One of Clover's legs crumpled beneath her and the horse quickly lost balance. Boudica tried to hold on with her knees but it was no good. She flew off and landed with a thump. The air was punched out of her and her left thigh was badly bruised but she staggered to her feet and ran after the horse.

Clover had slowed down but something wasn't right.

She looked terribly lopsided. Boudica called to her gently, "Clover, I'm so sorry. Come here."

There was a thud of hooves and a heavily built man with strong arms tattooed with blue dye jumped down from his horse. His tumbling red beard was sprinkled with grey, and his green eyes were a perfect match for her own. It was Jodoc, Boudica's father.

"Are you hurt?"

"No, I'm fine, but look at my horse."

Clover was limping with a mournful look in her eyes.

"That animal's lame," said Jodoc. "It'll never gallop again. How could you be so stupid? You should never ride a horse that fast on rocky ground. What were you thinking?"

Boudica had no answer, but she realized that this was the worst possible start to her parents' visit. She'd wanted them to think she'd grown up in her year away, but all they would see was a foolish child.

3

THE other members of the Icenian party caught up with Boudica and her father. There was her mother, ten Iceni warriors and Princess Bridgette, Queen Cartimandua's only child. Like Boudica, she was twelve years old and had spent the last year away from her tribe, in Jodoc's household. Boudica avoided catching her eye. *She must think I'm a complete idiot*, she said to herself.

"Boudica, climb up behind Prince Godrig," ordered Jodoc. "You can't ride your horse."

A boy shuffled forward on his brown pony, making more than enough room for Boudica on the saddle. Her replacement in Canna, the youngest son of the king of the Iceni, was a pale, slight child with wrists so thin that he barely looked strong enough to handle his mount. Boudica scrambled up awkwardly holding the reins of the limping Clover in her left hand. She was mortified. Sitting behind a ten-year-old boy, even if he was a prince and pulling a lame horse, was not the glorious entry to Canna that she had envisaged.

"What were you doing, making such a fool of yourself?" scolded Boudica's mother, Dagma, when they were on their way. She was a handsome woman who took care of her appearance. Even on this long journey she'd stained her lips with berry juice and plaited her long brown hair. Her cheeks were pink with irritation as she spoke. "And look at you. You're covered in mud and grime. Is this any way to greet your parents?"

Boudica was too unhappy to respond, so she just shook her head.

The sun was setting beneath the trees and the temperature was dropping fast. Boudica hadn't noticed the chilly wind when she and Clover galloped up the hill, but now she regretted not bringing a fur. The Iceni were snugly wrapped in wolfskins; she had only a wool shawl. She clenched her teeth to stop them chattering and discreetly pulled the shawl a little tighter.

"Boudica," whispered Godrig, "my fleece will go round both us."

Miserably, she rearranged the warm skin.

They plodded down the valley in silence and then Dagma started grumbling again.

"I've a good mind to complain to Queen Cartimandua about this," she said to her husband. "We sent Boudica here to become an asset to her tribe, but she's wilder than ever. No girl I've trained would behave like that. Look at Princess Bridgette. She's a credit to me."

Boudica stole a glance at the pretty girl riding at the back of the party. Despite the wind, her hair was neatly tucked away and her fine clothes were unruffled and surprisingly free of mud after such a long ride. With her turned up nose and delicate mouth, Boudica had to admit that she looked every inch the princess.

"Dagma, keep your voice down! Remember Queen Cartimandua's daughter is with us," said Jodoc. "We must do nothing to upset the Brigantes. My clear instructions from King Antedios were that we should remain friendly at all times. And Boudica is *our* daughter. She brings shame on us not the other way round."

Dagma harrumphed.

"Jodoc, they should never have given her a horse like that. She's not ready. You've said so many times. It's just Queen Cartimandua's way of showing off her wealth. That mare must be worth a small fortune."

Boudica's heart sank. The forest was thinning out and they would soon come to the tall wooden fence that protected Canna. She couldn't put off telling them any longer.

"Father, Mother, Queen Cartimandua didn't give me Clover. I borrowed her ... without asking."

Her parents looked horrified. Princess Bridgette overtook her Icenian escort, and pulled up next to Boudica.

"I thought that was Clover," she said triumphantly. "Probas traded twenty sheep for her with a man from the Dobunni tribe just before I left. Mother was furious at the expense but she could see she was special."

Boudica looked at the ground. She already felt awful and Princess Bridgette wasn't helping.

"Mother will be heartbroken when she sees what's become of her," continued the princess. "Clover's irreplaceable."

"Right, that's enough," said Jodoc. "I'll sort this mess out later. Princess Bridgette, why don't you ride ahead and meet your mother? I can see her down there by the gate. I'm sure she's anxious to see you."

Bridgette smiled slyly at Boudica and pranced off. Once she was safely out of earshot Jodoc said, "Boudica, you were sent here to foster understanding between the Iceni and the Brigantes but instead you've embarrassed me and your tribe."

Boudica knew her father was speaking the truth and that he was disappointed in her. She was determined to make it up to him.

"Father, I'm sorry", she said. "It won't happen again. I promise, one day I'll make you and the Iceni proud of me."

Jodoc sighed.

"I hope you will, Boudica. I really do."

4

"CHEER up and take this over to the queen."

Hendra cut off several thick slabs of dripping meat from a roasting boar and passed them on a plate to Boudica.

"Quick now, I don't want it getting cold."

Over two hundred people were crowded into a large, thatched banqueting hall. Brigantes from all the villages surrounding the town of Canna had been summoned by Queen Cartimandua to honour the return of her only child, Princess Bridgette. Everyone was dressed in their finest clothes. The men had spiked their hair with chalk and the women wore brightly coloured tartan skirts and shawls pinned with extravagant brooches, and had their heaviest gold torcs round their necks.

In the centre of the grand hall was a round, stone wall, about two foot high and within it a circle of low wooden tables. These were reserved for warriors. Everyone else had to make do with finding a space where they could. The warriors' shields were propped up against the wall, signifying where they would be seated. Each shield was ornately decorated. Some were checked, others patterned with concentric circles, but the dominant design was of swirling lines of bronze, silver and gold. They glowed in the roaring fire, forming a shimmering backdrop to the feast.

To sit in that circle was the highest honour a tribe could bestow. Boudica looked at the occupants enviously – every important man in Canna was there as well as Jodoc and his warriors and just one woman, Queen Cartimandua. She was a warrior with her own magnificent scarlet and gold shield to prove it. Dagma had to make do with sitting behind her husband, outside the magical circle. Boudica looked at her mother smoothing the creases in her elegant linen dress and wondered whether she minded. *I would*, she thought. Ever since she could remember, she had dreamed of being invited to join the circle of warriors. Few women ever made it, but it was not impossible. The queen was living proof of that.

"I said, don't let it get cold," said Hendra impatiently, pointing at the pork.

"Sorry, I'll go now," said Boudica quickly.

Boudica should have been sitting with Prince Godrig and her mother, but earlier that evening Princess Bridgette had made sure that she couldn't. Jodoc had apologized for the injury to Clover and given Queen Cartimandua a magnificent gold bracelet in compensation. The queen grudgingly accepted Jodoc's generous gift but Princess Bridgette had gone on and on about Boudica's reckless riding so much that Cartimandua had decided she must be punished. She would serve them all at the feast; that would teach her a lesson. Boudica knew her father wasn't happy. It was hardly becoming for the daughter of an Icenian warrior to be handing round food like a peasant's child but, because of her, he was in no position to complain.

The slabs of pork smelled delicious but Boudica couldn't eat until everyone had been served. She passed the dish to the queen, determined not to show how humiliated she felt. At home, Chiomara, her closest friend, was often called upon to serve at feasts and Boudica thought no less of her for that. *There's no shame in it*, she told herself. But Princess Bridgette's irritating smirk and her father's pained look told a different story. Even little Prince Godrig couldn't look her in the eye. Chiomara's father was a poor farmer and she was the daughter of a warrior and that made all the difference.

Cartimandua prodded the meat with her fingers, crinkling her prominent nose disdainfully as she ran her eyes over the pork. Finally, after burrowing down to the bottom of the plate, inspecting every cut, she pulled a piece out and passed it to Jodoc.

"I honour your visit with our most succulent meat."

She licked her greasy fingers and then pulled out more for herself.

"You'll remember this lesson, Boudica," she said as she waved her on.

Hendra and Argent provided a steady stream of

dishes. Boudica passed round salted beef, salmon cooked with cumin and vinegar, pease pudding, curd, bread and endless flagons of mead. By midnight she was exhausted from the smoke and noise and the drunken calls for more drink. She still hadn't eaten and her stomach was aching. At last, Hendra produced a tray of honey-sweetened cakes. Supper was almost over.

Queen Cartimandua got to her feet and the room fell silent.

"Jodoc, it's time I thanked you for looking after Princess Bridgette this last year."

"Ma'am, it was a pleasure," said Jodoc. "Now, may I suggest that my daughter has done sufficient penance for her misdemeanour this afternoon. Can she join us for her supper?"

Smiling, Boudica took the plate of leftovers that Hendra had set aside for her and settled onto a glossy fur behind her father just outside the stone circle. She bit into a rib of congealing pork.

"I hear the southern tribes have been badly defeated by the Romans," her father was saying.

Boudica pricked up her ears. So the rumours that had been doing the rounds these last few days were true. The Romans had returned. They had come once before, eighty years ago, but the tribes of Britain had united to see them off.

"Yes," answered the queen.

"My king has requested that you inform him, through me, of your plans. Will you fight them?"

Queen Cartimandua shook her head so emphatically that her long gold earrings jangled.

"I won't have to. The Romans will never come this far north; they hate the cold. The southern tribes have been selling them slaves, cattle and grain for years. The idiots have supplied the army that's now defeated them. If you ask me, they've got what they deserve."

"The Iceni and the Brigantes have shown more sense," agreed Jodoc. "But now the Romans are here they may get a taste for our island. Perhaps it would be better to expel them before they get too comfortable. King Caradoc of the Trinovantes is trying to unite the tribes that are still free, before it's too late."

Queen Cartimandua spat out a bone.

"Caradoc?" she said. "The Romans have already defeated him. They say he ran off like a fawn at the first sight of their soldiers."

Jodoc nodded slowly. It looked to Boudica as if he were weighing carefully in his mind how to proceed.

"He was defeated, but he's learned much from that battle. He thinks if we all work together we could succeed."

Queen Cartimandua snorted in disbelief.

"Jodoc, give this message to your king and Caradoc. No Brigantian blood will be spilt to save the southern tribes. Do you understand?"

Boudica was surprised by the venom in the queen's voice.

"But aren't we all tribes of Britain?" she blurted out, without thinking. "Shouldn't we unite?"

The words were hardly out of her mouth before Dagma grabbed her tightly by the arm.

"Queen Cartimandua, I must apologize for my daughter's impertinence. It appears she has still not learned her lesson."

She found herself being pulled out of the hall into the freezing night air.

"How many times do I have to tell you to behave?" said her mother. "I despair of you. Tessa is to be married and you should be next, but no one will want you if you carry on like this."

"I don't want anyone to want me," said Boudica defiantly. Didn't her mother understand? A husband was the last thing she was interested in. A life of cooking, washing and polishing weapons might suit her sister, but it would not do for her.

Dagma was furious. Her full lips were pressed so hard together that the colour had drained from them.

"What have I done to deserve such a daughter? Boudica, when we get back home I am going to take you in hand. You will learn what your duty is or I will make your life miserable. Do I make myself understood?"

Boudica remained provocatively silent.

"Now get to your room. And stay there till we leave Canna."

"But that's in two days' time."

"That's right," said her mother. "It'll give you time to think and learn."

5

"ARE you ready?" called Dagma.

Boudica looked around the home she had shared with Hendra and Argent for the last year. Her corner looked surprisingly free of clutter now that her clothes were tied in a bundle. All that was left was the fur on which she had slept. She would wrap it round her legs to keep her warm on the long ride home.

"Come on, Cinnia," said Boudica. "You're going to see the world."

A small puppy yapped excitedly. The animal was a parting gift from Culann. He was wiry with grey hair and eager black eyes, part wolf, part dog. It was the first dog she had ever owned and Boudica was enchanted with him.

She pulled the deerskin rug aside. The Iceni were standing by their horses in the main town square.

"Ah, here you are at last," said her mother. "Go and say goodbye to Queen Cartimandua and we'll be on our way."

"Where is she?" asked Boudica.

"In her rooms. Quickly. Your father wants to make an early start."

Boudica hurried past several wattle huts, built snugly together to shelter each other from the wind. She looked around as if seeing the town for the first time instead of the last. She had spent a year here, learning the Brigantian ways. When she arrived everything had seemed strange. The food was spicy, the people's manners harsh, their accents hard to understand, but most of all she had been struck by the unrelenting cold. The last winter had been bitter. A freezing wind had swept down the mountains, finding gaps in every building. In Brigantian territory spring took for ever to creep across the brooding hills and summer seemed to pass in an instant. But it was the constant drizzle she would remember most. In winter her clothes felt damp for days on end. She was sure that was why the Brigantes were such a bad-tempered lot. If it hadn't been for Culann she would be leaving without a backwards glance.

The sky was grey and damp as the Iceni plodded up the valley leaving Canna behind them. The rain was light but in no time Boudica's clothes were soaked. She held Cinnia close under a fur to keep him warm for he was too young to chase along beside the horses.

By lunchtime they reached a fast flowing stream. Jodoc dismounted. In his long, tartan trousers and with a knife in his hand he waded into the freezing water and broke the blade on a pointed rock. The brittle metal snapped into two pieces and Jodoc threw them both downstream.

"Goddess Andraste, accept our offering and bless our journey."

Boudica's spirits soared. This was how her journey had started all those months ago and now she was returning home to the land where she belonged. They would have to travel east out of Brigantian territory and then south through Corieltauvian land before finally reaching the fertile plains of the Iceni. If they were lucky it would only take five days.

By the end of the first day the landscape had changed. The forbidding moors gave way to forest. In the middle of a clearing they passed a wooden statue of a man propped up on a rock. His mouth was full of jagged teeth and his eyes protruded horribly, but to Boudica the statue was a welcome sight for it marked the point where they passed out of Brigantian land.

Tall pine trees, towering into the sky, lined the bridle path.

"Father, this would be the perfect place for an ambush, don't you think?" asked Boudica as they trotted along.

"All Corieltauvian territory is like this. They are forest people. But don't worry, this is a peaceful time. It's not them we have to worry about."

"It's the Romans," said Boudica, tentatively finishing his unspoken thought. "Is that what you mean?"

"Yes, but don't worry. The Iceni will hold them off."

He smiled at her reassuringly. This was the first time she had seen him smile since Clover went lame. She remembered the present she had asked Culann to make.

She'd meant to give it to her father on their first night home, but this would be the perfect time.

"Father, I have something for you," she said, reaching into the pocket of her soaking woollen skirt.

Jodoc inspected the knife closely.

"The workmanship is wonderful. Thank you, Boudica." He patted her head affectionately and then tucked the knife into his leather belt.

They rode on in peaceful silence. At last, as the evening light faded, Jodoc pulled up in a woodland glade and said, "We'll camp here for the night."

After a brief rest when everyone stretched their stiff limbs after a day in the saddle, Jodoc began issuing orders to his men. Five of them disappeared into the forest, emerging with enough sticks to make three makeshift tents. The others collected ferns and bracken to keep the rain out. Boudica lined the tents with bearskins and then helped her mother light a fire and make a supper of thick porridge.

By the time the meal was over the sky was black. The Iceni were too weary to talk much. The only sound was that of flames spitting on damp wood.

"Time for bed. We'll leave at first light," said Jodoc. "Agron, you'll take the first watch."

Boudica watched Agron closely as he settled himself by the fire, for this was the man her parents had finally chosen to be her sister's husband. He was a hefty warrior with a long drooping moustache, closer in age to Jodoc than Tessa. Boudica couldn't help thinking that he didn't look much fun. In fact his face was set in a permanent scowl, as if he'd just caught a whiff of a nasty smell. She didn't envy Tessa at all.

"To bed, Boudica," said Dagma.

Boudica slipped under the bear skin in the tent she was sharing with her father and mother. Cinnia lay at her feet. After such a long day she expected to fall asleep straightaway, but somehow she couldn't settle. Needles from the pine trees carpeted the clearing. Despite the thick fur, one spiked her every time she moved. Outside she could hear the distant howls of wolves, but she knew the fire would keep them at bay.

The sharp crack of a twig snapping stopped her drifting off. Then there was another, this time closer. It sounded too heavy to be an animal. Her heart was beating loudly now. Who could it possibly be outside? They were miles from anywhere.

Cinnia growled.

"Shush!" said Boudica sharply.

She shook Jodoc.

"Father, there's someone outside," she whispered.

Instantly Jodoc was alert. Boudica could hear him feeling for his sword. Then he was crouching by the entrance to the shelter.

"Don't move," he whispered. "I'll see who's there."

6

BOUDICA crawled to the front of the makeshift tent, frantic to see what was happening outside. Cinnia was growling and snarling. She grabbed the puppy and held him tightly, one hand under his chest and the other round his muzzle to stop him yapping, and peered outside.

Her father and Agron were standing by the fire, their tattooed arms raised and brandishing swords. They were an impressive sight. Jodoc was tall with hair to his waist; Agron was strong and muscular. Both men looked battle-hardened and ready.

"Who's there?" Jodoc called out gruffly.

Somebody answered. It was a man with a distinctive voice, who spoke from the back of his throat, as if his nose were blocked.

"You have nothing to fear. I am a druid."

"What do you want?"

"I saw your fire and wondered if I might join you for the night."

The man walked out of the shadows. He certainly looked like one of the druid priests that wandered across Britain, for he was wearing a long white robe over blue leggings and his face was obscured by a hood.

Round his neck hung a silver necklace and pendant.

"Are you alone?" said Jodoc, lowering his sword just a little.

"You can see that I am."

The stranger answered each question slowly and concisely, giving as little away as possible.

"Well, what are you doing out at this time of night? It must be past midnight."

"It's full moon. It's an auspicious time for picking wild spinach."

"Are you from Flembun?" asked Agron. This was the last Corieltauvian village they had ridden through that day.

"No."

"From where, then?" Agron sounded exasperated.

"I finished my studies on the Isle of Mona in the spring. Since then I've been travelling."

As druids often spent many years moving between tribes before finally settling down, this explanation satisfied Jodoc. He extended his arm in welcome.

"Come and join us. You look frozen. What's your name?"

The druid knelt by the fire, warmed his hands and pushed back his hood to reveal long, grey hair which seemed a mismatch for his unlined face, for he was only in his early thirties.

"Bodvoc," he said after a pause.

"And how long were you on Mona?" asked Agron.

"Twelve years."

"Is that all?" said Jodoc. "Well done. I've known men who took over twenty years to become druids."

"You must have been there with Corann," said Agron. "He's the chief druid of the Iceni but before that he taught at Mona."

"Corann?" said Bodvoc slowly. "No, I don't think I knew a Corann, but then the college at Mona is large. One couldn't possibly know everyone."

"He specialized in teaching verses to novice students."

"No," answered Bodvoc curtly. "I already told you. I didn't know him."

There was an awkward silence.

"Let me get you some porridge," said Jodoc at last. "There's a little left over from supper."

"No, thank you," said the unexpected guest, "just a fire for the night."

The druid was travelling with only a small sack slung across his back. He seemed totally unprepared for a night in the open.

"Let me at least get you something to sleep on," said Jodoc and, raising his voice, he called out, "Boudica, bring a couple of furs."

Boudica put Cinnia down so she could reach for a bundle. As soon as he was free the puppy ran out of the tent and started racing around the stranger, barking and jumping up at him.

"Get away from me," said the druid.

"Don't worry, he's harmless," said Boudica, handing over the fur and picking up the overexcited Cinnia.

"You haven't trained it properly," Bodvoc said brusquely. "It ought to be taught friend from foe."

Surely the stranger could see that the puppy was far too young for that, thought Boudica, but she knew she mustn't criticize a druid so she retreated to her tent.

"Don't worry," she whispered to the puppy when she was safely out of earshot, "that horrible man will be gone by tomorrow."

But she was wrong. Early next morning, when the dawn sun had barely penetrated the gloomy forest her father came to wake her.

"Boudica, you'll ride with your mother today," he said. "Druid Bodvoc is joining us. He'll be sharing my horse."

7

A small crowd stood at the gates of Sinovix, the largest town in Icenian territory, waiting to greet the returning travellers. Boudica searched eagerly for the faces she most wanted to see – Tessa and Chiomara. She spotted the round, freckled face of her sister first, slipped off the saddle and ran over to hug her.

"I'm so glad you're back," said Tessa. "It's been a nightmare. I've had to put up with Princess Bridgette's airs and graces for twelve months."

"Really? Mother seems to think she's wonderful; a proper little woman and a credit to her tribe," said Boudica, perfectly imitating Dagma.

Tessa laughed. "Believe me, she was awful. We'll all be much happier now you're home." They linked arms. "Tell me, how was it?"

As they walked into the town Boudica recounted the highs and the lows of the last year but they seemed like stories from another time now that she was home. What she really wanted to know was what had been happening while she'd been away.

"I hear mother finally picked a warrior for you?" she said tentatively, not sure how Tessa would feel about Agron.

"Yes. You know who it is?"

Boudica nodded. From the moment Tessa had turned fourteen, Dagma had been indiscreetly running her eye over every warrior who crossed her path.

"He seems like a good man," was the best comment Boudica could offer.

"I hope so."

"But you must delay the marriage as long as possible," Boudica told her with a smile. "As long as you're unwed she won't be looking for a husband for me. Oh look, there's Chiomara. I must say hello."

Chiomara was almost exactly Boudica's age. She was slight but strong. From the day she'd learnt to walk she'd worked from dawn to dusk on the family farm, and consequently her fair hair was sun-streaked and her skin tanned.

"I wanted to be the first to meet you but I wasn't sure when you were coming," she said breathlessly. "Your mother wouldn't tell me."

"Don't worry," said Boudica.

She didn't care if Chiomara was first or not, she was just happy to see her. In no time they were chatting and joking as if they'd last seen each other earlier that morning rather than a year before. Chiomara updated her on all the gossip and when she finished she asked, "By the way, who's that druid?"

She was pointing at Bodvoc, who was being introduced to people by Jodoc on the opposite side of the town square.

"Oh, that's Bodvoc," said Boudica. "We met him in the woods four nights ago. He seemed to sneak up on us. To tell you the truth, he gives me the creeps. Ever since he joined us he's been sidling up to everyone, asking nosy questions. Even mother got fed up with him and she likes druids."

Boudica was laughing at the comical way her mother fawned over Corann, the chief druid to the Iceni, when she felt a tap on the shoulder.

"It's time to be getting home," said Dagma sharply. "Chiomara, Boudica's going to be very busy for the next few weeks so you won't be able to see her for some time."

"But I was planning to go to the farm this afternoon," protested Boudica.

Why did her mother always make things so difficult? Dagma had been stubbornly against Chiomara since the day they'd met. Although it was over seven summers ago Boudica still remembered it. Belos, Chiomara's father, had come to Sinovix with wool to trade, carrying her on his shoulders. She had looked tiny compared to her huge bear of a father.

Boudica had asked Dagma who they were, for it wasn't often that strangers came into the town.

"They've planted fields at the bottom of the valley but his wife died just before that wool was cut. Stay away; the girl could carry bad luck."

Boudica had stared curiously at the little girl, looking

for signs of the misfortune her mother was so worried about, but she seemed ordinary enough. Chiomara had noticed the attention she was getting and stared back. Suddenly she'd stuck out a little pink tongue and smiled. It had made Boudica laugh and from then on whenever Boudica saw her in the town she would say hello. In no time they were friends, but Dagma's hostility was unwavering. Chiomara was not just unlucky, she was poor as well and it was unbecoming to the family for Boudica to associate with her. Boudica should concentrate on growing into a lady like her sister, Tessa.

"Mother," Boudica pleaded, "can't I go just this once?"

"Certainly not – we've only just got back. There's far too much to be done."

Boudica did a quick calculation. Her mother would be watching her like a hawk for the next week or so. It would be pointless trying to get away, but then she would tire of it and Boudica would get her chance.

"I'll see you at the well at midday in two weeks," Boudica mouthed at Chiomara as she left, and she held up two fingers just to make sure it was clear.

Chiomara nodded and smiled. They both understood. Things were going to be just as they had been before Boudica left for her year with the Brigantes – cat and mouse with Dagma.

It was two weeks since Boudica's return home. Dagma

was busy in the market and Jodoc was visiting King Antedios. While Tessa was up a ladder hanging hams to cure in the smoke above the fireplace, Boudica took her chance. She kicked over a jar of water that was used for cooking.

"Oops, I'd better go and fill it up again."

Before Tessa had time to say that there was plenty more water, Boudica was out of the house. She skirted round the marketplace and, when she was sure that she hadn't been spotted, ducked through the town gates and ran without stopping all the way to the well with Cinnia at her heels.

The well was only a hundred feet from the edge of a sacred wood and by the time she reached it Boudica was out of breath. She sat down and looked up at the sun. It wasn't even close to midday; she was far too early, but she would wait for Chiomara, however much trouble she got into when she returned home. Dagma would guess what she was up to, after all Sinovix had a spring just outside the town walls and she could have filled the jar there, but her mother forced her to behave like this by being so unreasonable.

Cinnia dropped a stick at Boudica's feet. She picked it up and, as it was wet with saliva, quickly tossed it away. It landed just inside the sacred oak forest. Boudica hadn't meant to throw it that way but Cinnia couldn't know that. He disappeared into the dense wood and after a while she heard him yapping in frustration. He must be having difficulties finding it but she couldn't help him. On holy days, the spirits of the dead were said to return to the wood. Magical plants with healing properties grew there and wild creatures, carrying messages from the gods, roamed freely. It was a dangerous, mysterious place that was strictly forbidden to anyone but the druids.

At the top of the valley a figure in a long cloak caught Boudica's eye. It must be Dagma. All the frustrations of the last ten days boiled over. Her mother had filled her time with tedious chores that Princess Bridgette, apparently, did without complaining – washing, weaving, peeling vegetables and dyeing clothes. At last she had the chance to be outside, doing what she wanted to do, and her mother was going to ruin it again. *Well I won't let her*, thought Boudica. Impulsively she took refuge in the only place where she knew her mother would never find her – the sacred oak forest. Could it really be so terrible to slip behind the thick trunk of the outermost tree?

Cinnia was still snuffling around. Boudica whistled and the dog ambled over. She picked him up, holding him close. All was quiet around her. Even the birds were silent. She peeped out from behind the trunk. The figure was heading straight for the forest and as it came closer Boudica realized that it wasn't Dagma, for the cloak was white with a distinctive pointy hood and a brim that obscured the face. This kind of cloak was only worn by druids, and if one of them found her in the forest, breaking their strict rules, she would be expelled from her tribe for ever. However senior her father was, he wouldn't be able to stop it. She must have been mad.

Boudica stood as still as possible and thanked the gods she was wearing a mud-brown dress that would help camouflage her. Cinnia seemed to understand the precariousness of the situation and, for once, didn't wriggle. Boudica listened as intently as she could for footsteps but there was no sound.

Slowly she shifted her weight to her left foot and looked cautiously round the tree trunk. There, only twenty feet away, was Druid Bodvoc glancing furtively over his shoulder. One look at his face told her he was doing something he didn't want anyone else to know about. She knew why *she* shouldn't be here, but why on earth would a druid be worried? Suddenly she was certain that Bodvoc was up to no good and, without thinking, she began to follow him.

8

BODVOC moved further into the forest. Whenever Druid Corann made trips into the sacred wood he would emerge with bags weighed down with herbs and bark, but Bodvoc didn't look like a man searching for anything; he was in too much of a hurry for that.

Keeping a safe distance, darting from tree to tree, Boudica followed him. She could feel her heart racing, as she went deeper and deeper in. The forbidden wood was home to spirits and ghosts and terrifying animals that only the druids knew how to tame. So far it looked no different from any other forest, but Boudica knew there were things here that she didn't understand. Could the gods be luring her in to punish her for her impertinence? Quickly, she pushed the thought to the back of her mind.

The ground began sloping steeply. Here the trees grew closer together, little sunlight penetrated, and the earth was bare. At the bottom of the gully was a murky stream, too wide to jump and too muddy to wade through. From a safe distance Boudica watched Bodvoc approach a lone tree that had fallen across the gorge. On this side its roots were exposed. They were covered with mushrooms and moss, filling the forest with the pungent smell of rotting vegetation. She watched him climb the tree: for such a tall man his movements were surprisingly fluid.

Boudica didn't like Bodvoc. She was sure he was up to something and she wanted to find out what. So far she had acted instinctively but the fallen tree forced her to make a decision. She could turn round and no one but the gods would ever know that she had broken a terrible taboo and entered the forest. But if she crossed that stream, there would be no going back. She paused, unsure of what to do, and then Bodvoc glanced behind him once more. There was that furtive look again. Boudica made up her mind. She pulled up her skirt, picked up Cinnia, and began climbing.

The trunk was slippery. Carefully she inched her way across, grabbed a branch, swung down to the ground and then scrambled up the bank on the other side.

The trees began to thin a little. Boudica was relieved. She was almost through the forest. Beyond the wood she could see a trail riddled with hoof marks, which she recognized as the lonely bridle path that skirted the far side of the sacred wood then wound its way to the distant coast. Why would Bodvoc be in such a hurry to get here? The druid was sitting on his haunches, leaning against the outermost tree trunk, staring at the path. A single rider came over the brow of the hill and immediately Bodvoc jumped to his feet and whistled shrilly. The rider must have been expecting this for he trotted over. He was dressed in a long bright blue tunic and a greasy cape decorated with geometric embroidery, and his face looked as if it had been stained with berry juice. From his colouring and his clothing Boudica knew that he wasn't a Briton. He reminded her of a merchant who had once come to Sinovix selling peculiar remedies all the way from Gaul.

The stranger jumped down from his horse and led it into the wood where he and Bodvoc began an animated conversation. Frustratingly, they were too far away for Boudica to hear, but as she hid behind a tree she realized why Bodvoc had been in such a hurry. The bridle path was the only route into Sinovix which couldn't be seen from the town. He'd planned this meeting and he didn't want anyone else to know.

The men's conversation seemed to go on and on, but the stranger was facing into the forest and any movement would catch his eye. Boudica would just have to wait until they'd finished.

A pheasant strolled by, pecking aimlessly at the ground. Boudica felt Cinnia tense, then twist and turn, trying to get away from her, but she held him tight. He yowled in frustration.

"Shush now," Boudica whispered, shooing the silly bird away, but the excitement was too much for Cinnia who yelped again.

"Not now," she said urgently.

The wretched puppy was now barking as loudly as he

could. Boudica tried clamping her hand round his muzzle but he wriggled free. Desperately, she peeped out from behind the tree trunk. Bodvoc and the stranger were walking in her direction to investigate the noise. She mustn't stay a moment longer. She picked up her skirt and ran as fast as she could, with Cinnia following close behind.

Her hem got caught up in a bramble. She felt it rip but pushed on. As long as she kept going she had a good chance of outrunning Bodvoc and she must. If she was caught the punishment would be terrible. What had possessed her to be so stupid?

Ahead of her she saw the fallen tree at the bottom of the ravine. She scrambled down the damp slope, sending the crumbly earth skidding. Nimbly she used her hands to keep balance. She was out of breath and her side ached from the effort but she could not allow herself to stop. Bodvoc didn't have to catch up; he just had to get close enough to recognize her. As she clambered up the branches of the fallen tree onto the trunk that traversed the muddy stream, she allowed herself one quick glance behind. Bodvoc wasn't in the ravine yet. She'd done it! But in that moment she lost her concentration and her foot slipped on the rotting wood, sending her tumbling down. She landed awkwardly in the fetid mud. Dazed and winded, all she could see was Cinnia panicking above her. He was standing on the tree trunk, yapping at the top of his voice, not sure whether to jump down to her or cross to the other side.

"Go on, you silly dog," said Boudica.

Cinnia jumped and came skittering down to his mistress.

They had to get going again – Bodvoc would be coming into the ravine at any moment. Bodica's woollen skirt, heavy with filthy sludge, was bound to slow her down but she must try. She attempted to get to her feet but a searing pain in her left leg stopped her.

Oh no, she thought. *Please, not this. Not now.*

She tried to move again but the pain too great. She'd hurt her ankle in the fall. She was stuck. The gods *were* punishing her.

9

BOUDICA sat in the mud waiting for Bodvoc to find her. She was scared, of course, but her overwhelming emotion was one of fury. If only she'd been more careful she might have got out of this mess.

Cinnia started growling. He must have caught the scent of the druid.

"Stop it," said Boudica automatically.

Even as she spoke, she knew it was pointless; a yap here or there wasn't going to make any difference. In any event Cinnia would not be quieted. As if possessed he barked and barked and ran backwards and forwards along the bank of the stream. Then, just as Bodvoc appeared at the top of the ravine, he shot off into the trees, howling. Boudica's spirits sank. Even Cinnia had abandoned her. She glanced up to see how far away Bodvoc was. The druid had stopped moving. He was standing absolutely still, listening to Cinnia's demented yowls. He must think the sound would lead to whoever was following him, thought Boudica, and instantly she realized Bodvoc hadn't seen her fall. He didn't know where she was. Whether Cinnia knew it or not, he was acting as a perfect decoy, distracting the druid from paying too much attention to the stream. The puppy had given her a chance and she had to take it.

Quickly Boudica sat up and shuffled forward, trying desperately to get under the fallen tree before Bodvoc reached the crossing. She used her arms to pull herself but it was impossibly hard work – her hands kept sinking into the gooey mud.

"Come on," she said, willing herself more strength.

Her body inched forwards. She was shaking from the effort but she had less than a foot to go. Her ankle bumped over a stone in the stream but she ignored the pain. The water was freezing and foul smelling but in this gloomy spot she might just pass unnoticed.

With one last push she was under the trunk just as the branches creaked from the weight of a man. She could hear Bodvoc's footsteps. Now he was directly above her. Thank goodness for her brown skirt; she blended perfectly with her surroundings. She sat still. He seemed to be taking an eternity to cross and then there was a thud on the far side of the bank and the druid chased off after Cinnia's barks.

Boudica felt like whooping for joy.

By the time Boudica had limped home the sun had set. Dagma and Jodoc were frantic with worry; too frantic to question her convoluted explanation of how she had tripped on the way to the well. Tessa helped her out of her sodden clothes and laid her down by the fire under a fur, but even its weight on her leg was agony. Tired as she was, she could only sleep fitfully. Each time she closed her eyes she was sucked back into the forest. Except this time there was no escaping. Wolves were on her trail; Bodvoc had her in a snare. She was stuck in the mud. It was pulling her down deeper and deeper.

A voice penetrated her wild dreams.

"Boudica, your ankle is broken. I'm going to have to reset your leg. Do you understand?"

Slowly she opened her eyes. She wasn't in the wood at all. She was in her own home and there was the kindly face of Corann, the chief druid. He was crouched next to her bed with her parents and Tessa watching anxiously behind. The only light came from the remains of a fire in the hearth. It must be the middle of the night. She tried to move but the pain in her calf stopped her.

"Keep still and drink this."

Boudica was too woozy to object. The liquid was grey and tasted hideously sour. She tried to spit it out but Corann put his hand over her mouth and tilted her head so that the bitter concoction trickled down her throat.

"Boudica, try to relax, do you understand?" said Corann in his familiar, soothing tones.

She wanted to nod but was too quickly enveloped in sleep.

"When will she wake up?"

It was her mother speaking.

"Some time this morning, but she'll need to stay in bed for several days while her leg heals."

And that was Corann.

Boudica pulled herself up onto her elbows, pale from the effort of even this small movement. Something odd had happened to her bed. There was a large lump at the bottom.

"Ah, earlier than I expected," said Corann. "How is the patient?"

Boudica's head was more painful than anything else.

"Fine," she said, her voice betraying how weak she was really feeling. "What's that?"

"Your father made it from willow and hazel branches. It's to keep the blankets off your leg. They seemed to be disturbing you in the night."

"How long have I been asleep?"

"A day and a half. I expect you have a headache."

Boudica nodded.

"As I was saying to your mother, you will need to keep still for at least ten days, and then I will come and take another look. It could be some time before you can walk again, but you were lucky. The fracture was straightforward and you're young. It should heal well. I think you'll be up in time for the festival of Beltaine."

Boudica's head felt too heavy to lift. She lay back down.

"Thank you," she murmured as she drifted off into another deep sleep.

10

TOGETHER, Tessa and Dagma made sure Boudica followed Druid Corann's instructions. At first she was not allowed out of bed and could put no weight on her foot at all. To begin with she was so exhausted that she was content to lie around and doze, but after a few days she became frustrated. Dagma tried to occupy her with chores. Her foot propped up on a log near the fire, Boudica chopped vegetables, patched a cloak and spun the new wool. The tasks were tedious and did little to raise her spirits.

Early one morning Jodoc came and crouched by her bed.

"You're bored, aren't you?"

Boudica nodded. She certainly was.

"Begill's baby will be one next week," said her father. "See if you can start a doll for me. I'll finish it off this evening."

He handed over a block of wood and a knife. Boudica sat up. This was more interesting. She started chipping away at the block, but the knife kept slipping from her hand. Its handle was made for an adult, not for her smaller fingers.

Jodoc came back to see how she was getting on. He

watched her struggle for a while and then said, "How about using this?"

From inside his belt he pulled out the knife that she'd given him after her year with the Brigantes.

"Thanks," she said, "I'll give it back tonight."

The miniature dagger was much easier to handle and Boudica made good progress. The work was slow but absorbing and she hardly noticed the time pass. By sunset a head and body were recognizable.

Tessa returned from feeding the pigs.

"We've got a visitor, so please behave."

Boudica could see she was nervous.

"Who is it?" she asked.

"Agron."

The warrior stooped low to pass through the wattle door and came and sat by the fire. He sniffed the air and scowled.

"What's cooking?"

"Roast hedgehog," said Tessa quietly.

"You're doing it?"

"Yes."

"Good. I need a wife that can cook. The last one was dreadful."

He spat into the fire to emphasize the point. Boudica saw Tessa wince. Her sister seemed completely tongue-tied.

"My ankle's healing well," Boudica piped up, to stop the silence from becoming too awkward. "I should be walking by Beltaine, and in the meantime Father has asked me to make a doll."

"You haven't got very far with it, have you?" said Agron.

"No, but it's better now I'm using this." She held up the knife that Culann had made. "I gave it to Father," she said proudly, "and now he wears it all the time."

"All the time, does he?"

Boudica seemed to have found something that interested Agron but just then, thankfully, Dagma returned. Her mother would be much better at entertaining the dreary warrior. Dagma was carrying three fat legs of salted pork which she dumped on the floor.

"Were you after Jodoc?" she asked Agron.

"No, just checking up on Tessa. I'll be off now."

"Seems as if everyone's interested in us today," said Dagma once Agron had left. "I met Bodvoc, the new druid, in the square, and he asked me all about Boudica's leg."

Boudica felt the colour drain from her face. Bodvoc asking about her could not be good.

"I told him Corann is looking after you perfectly well," continued Dagma, oblivious to the effect her words were having on her daughter, "but he still wanted to know exactly how and where you hurt yourself. He was very particular about it."

Boudica was horrified. It could only mean one thing – Bodvoc must have suspicions about her.

"Are you all right?" asked Tessa. "You look very pale."

"I'm fine," said Boudica. "Honestly."

She picked up the doll and started scratching away at it but her hand was shaking too much to carve anything.

11

DAGMA carefully smeared purple berry juice onto her lips in front of a polished shield. It was the finishing touch to her finest outfit – a checked dress and matching stole both made from the softest wool. Her hair was held in a bun with gold clips and on each shoulder was a handsome brooch studded with gemstones.

"Boudica, are you ready yet?"

"Yes."

Her mother turned round.

"You can't go like that," she said, exasperation creeping into her voice. "Your hair needs a comb and that dress is too plain. Put something colourful on; it's important to remind people who you are."

Boudica rolled her eyes. This was her first opportunity to leave the house since breaking her ankle. Corann had said she would not be better before the festival of Beltaine and her impatience had done nothing to change that. But at last she was strong enough to walk, even if it was with a crutch. She didn't care whether her skirt called attention to her father's wealth or not, she just wanted to get going, but her mother was resolute. This was the highlight of the year, the festival that ensured summer followed winter, and she must look smart.

Boudica changed her beige skirt for a tartan one with bold squares of blue, red and green. She pinned a fresh shawl round her shoulders and pulled her wild locks into a ponytail. Meanwhile, Tessa poured water on the hearth. It hissed and steamed but the embers still glowed. The festival of Beltaine could only begin when every flame in the town was extinguished so that the spirits could not see to make mischief during the ceremony.

"Here, let me try," said Boudica. She dipped a large rag in the remains of the water and dropped it on the cinders. "It's fine now."

They all went out into the chill night air. Although summer was coming, the temperature plummeted once the sun slipped below the horizon. Boudica, walking slowly and leaning on a crutch, pulled her wrap closer. The swelling in her ankle had gone, but even so it felt strange to be putting any weight on her left leg, which was weak and made her feel awkward and lopsided.

The only light came from the waxing moon. They joined the crowd waiting at the entrance to the temple in the town square. The temple gates stood in the middle of a high oak fence surrounded by a ditch several feet deep, packed with bones, glowing chalky white in the moonlight. There were sheep skulls, cow horns and great long horse ribs.

Dagma stamped her feet to stop them from getting cold.

"I do wish they'd get on with it. I'm freezing," she complained.

At last, just when it was beginning to drizzle, the gates creaked open and the Iceni filed across a narrow bridge into the temple. A sacrifice had not been made for several weeks and so most of the carcasses in the gruesome ditch had been picked clean by ravens and crows. Even so, Boudica held her breath as there was still a lingering smell of rotten flesh.

Once inside the temple courtyard, Boudica looked around for Chiomara. Between breaking her ankle and her mother's vigilance, Boudica had still not managed to see her friend and it was driving her mad. Chiomara would be standing at the back with the other farmers and their children. Her father, Belos, was abnormally tall and should be easy to spot, but Boudica couldn't see him anywhere.

"Get a move on," said Dagma. "You're holding people up; King Antedios is coming."

As the family of a senior warrior, Dagma and her daughters were always seated towards the front. Boudica had no choice but to move forward.

The courtyard was dominated by an unlit bonfire, a tangled mass of rowan branches that had been specially collected from the sacred wood and dried over the last month. The beacon was so huge that it obscured the front of the temple, the largest building in the town. Its walls were made from wattle and two granite pillars, weathered to a silvery grey, supported a stone lintel marking the entrance. Only druids and warriors could cross this threshold.

King Antedios walked up the aisle that divided the courtyard accompanied by his eldest son Prince Prasutagus. Prasutagus was nothing like his younger brother, the delicate Prince Godrig. He was a tall, broadshouldered man with high cheekbones and a scar from his hairline to his left eyebrow. Boudica was struck by how old the king looked in comparison to his vigorous son. Antedios slowly made his way through the crowd, leaning heavily on Prasutagus and then stopped when he reached the front row of benches.

"It's always good when an Icenian child returns to the tribe," said the king. "You fared well with the Brigantes?"

Boudica smiled and nodded.

"And you're finally up and about, I see," said a nasal voice.

In the dimness Boudica hadn't noticed Bodvoc standing behind the king. He was the last person she wanted to see. She had tried and tried to put that terrible trip into the forest out of her mind, but seeing him brought it back more clearly than ever. If only he would go on his travels like other druids, and leave her alone.

"Yes, she's almost better," said Dagma.

"How *did* you break that ankle?" the king asked Boudica.

"I slipped, sir, on some mud near a well," Boudica answered, trying to sound as unflustered as possible.

Bodvoc raised his eyebrows. His expression was impossible to decipher. It might convey disbelief, surprise or condolence.

"Boudica, would you jump the embers with me tonight?" he asked.

Jumping the embers of the Beltaine fire ensured good health for the following year and was an auspicious time for making wishes. Boudica had been planning to do this with Chiomara, not Bodvoc. She wanted to be as far away from him as possible, but before she could think of an excuse, King Antedios said, "Well, Boudica, what an honour! It's good luck to start the New Year jumping with a druid."

He smiled kindly at her. Boudica tried to smile back but her knees felt as if they would buckle and she sat down heavily in her seat.

"Bodvoc, I think Boudica is quite overcome with your offer," said the king. "Now let's get started."

12

BOUDICA sat between Dagma and Tessa. Outwardly she looked calm but her mind was humming. She was going to have to jump the embers with Bodvoc, but why? What could he possibly want with her?

Druid Corann emerged from the temple dressed in a robe of pristine white wool with a chain of silver discs round his waist. In one hand he held a bunch of mistletoe to bring fertility in the coming year and in the other a burning torch. This was now the only light in the whole town. He held the flickering flame aloft.

"Before the festivities begin, King Antedios wishes to speak."

The king got to his feet and spoke painfully slowly. He seemed exhausted by the effort and kept pausing in odd places to take a breath.

"Many of you have come ... tonight not just to celebrate Beltaine ... but also to hear news of the Romans. I'm afraid ... that news is disturbing. King Caradoc of the Trinovantes has ... been defeated. His tribe was butchered – there is no other word for it. Anyone who survived ... is now a slave and the Romans ... are camping in his capital, Camulodunon, less than a day's ride from here."

A nervous murmur went around the temple courtyard.

"The question we must answer tonight," continued Antedios, gathering a little speed, "is should we be the next tribe to try and defeat the Romans? The Brigantes will not fight. They are convinced that the Romans will not come this far north but, I ask myself, how can we be sure?"

He shrugged his shoulders.

"I don't wish to spill Icenian blood by picking an unnecessary fight but, on the other hand, the Romans may be battle-weary. This might be our best chance to defeat them. I have discussed this dilemma at length with both Corann and the visiting druid, Bodvoc."

Not him again, thought Boudica. *That man meddles in everything.*

"Bodvoc told me that last night he had a dream."

There was a frisson of excitement. The Iceni understood the power of dreams. Only last summer Corann had dreamt that a traveller could bring trouble to the tribe, so King Antedios had not allowed any stranger into Icenian territory for thirty days. In that time a swelling sickness had spread across the land but no one in Sinovix caught the illness.

"Andraste, Goddess of Victory, came to him in the night and told him that a hare would be found in the sacred oak wood that would guide us. This afternoon Bodvoc caught a young buck in the grove. We will now learn what this hare has to tell us."

Bodvoc turned round and picked up a large sack and held it up for everyone to see. Once disturbed the sack began swinging wildly.

"If the hare runs to the west, Andraste is telling you to make war on the Romans," announced the druid in his dull nasal tones. "If it runs to the east, you should remain at home."

Boudica's eyes, like every other Icenian's, were now glued to the bag. The future of the tribe rested on it. War or peace, soon they would all know.

Bodvoc put the bag on the ground, reached in and grabbed the animal. He set it down at his feet. The hare still had its thick winter coat of grey fur. Its long ears were bolt upright and its beady eyes wild and terrified. Given the slightest chance it would spring away.

The druid whispered into the hare's ear and then theatrically sprung it free. The frightened animal dashed off, swinging immediately to the left. But then, confused by the crowd, the hare twisted right. It circled, came back towards the king and then turned again, at last finding the path that led to the gate and freedom.

All this happened in a matter of seconds. The crowd at the back of the temple ran after it, watching to see which direction it would choose. Shouts could be heard from outside.

"It's going west."

"It disappeared in that dip, where the sun sets."

"This means war."

Bodvoc banged two sticks together, demanding silence. "Why do you say war," he complained, "when you all saw that its first step was to the east? Do you not want to receive the message that the gods sent you?"

Boudica was surprised. Jodoc had often told her that a hare would dart this way or that in the temple, but it was outside in the fields, when it was free, that counted.

There were murmurings of disapproval. She was not the only one who was perturbed by the new druid's interpretation.

King Antedios raised his hands, demanding silence.

"Bodvoc found the hare. The sign was given to him so we must follow his ruling. Corann, please begin the Beltaine fire."

Boudica watched distractedly as the old druid chanted, blew horns, waved the torch and mistletoe and, at last, pushed both into the bonfire. Once the fire was burning fiercely its ashes were raked into a hot carpet. When it was ready Boudica felt a hand tighten on her shoulder and propel her towards the glowing embers.

"What will you wish for tonight?"

It was the grating voice she had been dreading – Bodvoc. With his pallid eyes that gave nothing away, grey hair, beard and white robe he was strangely devoid of colour.

"I want Andraste to teach me to become a warrior," answered Boudica truthfully.

She expected Bodvoc to laugh at her presumption but he merely nodded and led her to the flames. Already people were jumping either alone or in pairs. The heat was intense.

"Don't you want to know what I am going to wish for?" asked Bodvoc as they waited their turn. His lips were turning upwards but it was hard to call it a smile. It made her skin crawl. They were standing only a foot away from the cinders which glowed in every shade of red, orange and yellow. She could feel their singeing heat. Before she could answer, Bodvoc grabbed her hand.

"I wish all children to obey our rules."

The words had hardly sunk in before he leapt, tugging hard on her hand and pulling her with him. She was so surprised that she half stumbled on her crutch before she jumped. It meant that her leap wasn't as long as it should have been and her heel landed on hot ash. Quickly she stamped her foot on wet grass. Without checking whether she was all right Bodvoc disappeared into the crowd, but he had left something for her. In that moment when he'd taken her hand, he'd pressed something soft into it.

She knelt down near the fire so that she could see what it was and her stomach tightened horribly. In her hand was a piece of cloth, a scrap of muddy, brown linen that must have been ripped from her skirt by a bramble in the forest.

13

THAT night Boudica lay in bed unable to sleep, going over and over what had happened with Bodvoc. He had trapped her into jumping with him and as good as told her that he knew she'd followed him into the forbidden forest. Clearly he had planned it all, but she was still mystified. Why didn't he just tell Jodoc?

She rolled onto her side.

"Boudica, go to sleep," said a tired voice next to her. It was Tessa.

"Sorry," whispered Boudica.

She tried to lie still but she couldn't stop her mind from whirring. Would Bodvoc report her to Druid Corann or, worse still, the king? Would he demand something of her in return for his silence? But it had been more than fifteen days since she had followed him and if he was going to do any of those things, surely he would have done them by now. Maybe that was the end of it, she thought, trying to comfort herself, and yet she felt uneasy. Why let her off so easily? It was all very odd.

At last she fell asleep but it was a fitful, troubling night. With the first shaft of sunlight she got up and slipped out of the house, carrying her moccasins. None of the family stirred. Only Cinnia woke up, stretched his front legs and ambled after her.

The sun looked like a golden disc through the early morning haze. There was no one about and as soon as Boudica was in the fresh air, she felt her worries recede a little. All she needed was some time away from the cramped, one room house. A walk to Chiomara's farm would be perfect and at last she would see her friend.

"Come on, Cinnia, you'll enjoy this," said Boudica as she headed towards the town gate.

She found she was able to walk quite briskly and she hardly put any weight on her crutch. In a few days, hopefully, she would be able to do without it altogether.

As she crossed a field someone caught her up. It was Druid Corann, carrying a wicker basket. For an old man, he was remarkably sprightly.

"You're up early," he said cheerfully. "Off to see Chiomara, before your mother wakes?"

Boudica nodded happily. She knew that Corann wouldn't say a word.

"Well, good to see you on your feet again. Have fun. I'm off to the sacred forest; dawn is the best time for mushrooms."

Boudica cut across a wheat field to Chiomara's home. It was a dejected-looking building – the thatched roof was patchy and the wattle needed attention. Smoke was rising through the central chimney though so somebody must be up. She cupped her hands and hooted: it was her usual way of calling Chiomara.

As soon as she saw her friend, Boudica knew something was wrong. Chiomara was unusually pale, her complexion matching her straw-coloured hair, and she looked terribly thin.

"What's the matter?"

"Father's ill, I've been nursing him," said Chiomara tearfully. "Boudica, he needs help. I think it's the swelling sickness."

A couple of years ago, the tribe had been ravaged by an illness which seemed to choose its victims at random. Prince Godrig's mother, the queen, had been struck down and died within seven days. A person would complain of feeling stiff one day and by the next their arms and legs were so engorged that they were impossible to bend. Boudica was revolted at the thought of Belos in such a state but she did her best to hide it; sympathy was what Chiomara needed, not disgust.

"How bad is he?" she asked once she was sure her voice would not betray her.

"I don't know – bad. He tosses and turns day and night and he can't keep any food down and he says that his arms and legs ache."

"So there's no swelling yet?"

"No. But it could start at any time. You know how it is."

Boudica nodded.

"Has he seen a medicine man?"

"We can't afford that," said Chiomara without bitterness. It was a statement of fact. Belos could barely afford to keep them in food and clothes.

"What about Druid Corann? Have you spoken to him?"

Chiomara shook her head.

"I can't go to him. We're just poor farmers..."

"Boudica!" a voice called. "Boudica! Come here!"

Boudica turned around to see her mother standing at the top of the valley that dropped down to the farm.

"Listen, I have to go. But don't worry. I'll go and ask Corann for help and I'll get him to come to you as soon as I can."

"How many times do I have to tell you to stay away from Chiomara?" asked Dagma as Boudica approached. "She's just a peasant. Her father has nothing. You will never marry a decent warrior if you're always seen hanging around with people like that."

"She's my friend," protested Boudica.

"Not any more," retorted Dagma firmly.

We'll see about that, thought Boudica furiously. *We'll see about that.*

Late that morning she slipped out of the house. She had spotted Corann coming back from the sacred forest with a basket overflowing with mushrooms and muddy sticks. He would now be sorting the things he had collected into those that needed drying and those that needed preserving in oil or salt. It was the perfect time to ask for help.

The sun was still high in the sky. At this time the square was usually dotted with people, but today it was deserted. They must still be recovering from Beltaine, thought Boudica. Good. It wasn't that she was forbidden from going into the temple compound but it was something she would never ordinarily do by herself and she didn't want anyone to stop her.

She crossed the ditch of bones and knocked on the temple gate. Tentatively she called out, "Druid Corann?"

There was no answer. She glanced behind her; still nobody about. She pushed on the gate and it swung open.

"Druid Corann," she called again as she slipped inside.

The courtyard was empty except for a cow penned in a corner paddock whose carcass would soon join the grisly remains in the ditch. Judging by her mournful eyes, she sensed her fate.

The gate clicked shut. The ground was scarred black by the Beltaine fire and beyond the scorched earth was the granite doorway to the temple itself. Corann must be in there. The courtyard seemed enormous now that Boudica was its only occupant. She walked cautiously towards the temple.

"Druid Corann?" she called out. "It's me, Boudica."
Silence.

He must be here, she thought, *I saw him only moments ago.*

The glossy bearskin rug that covered the door rippled in the breeze. She realized that the rug would probably deaden any sound, but she couldn't just pull it aside. Entering the forest was bad enough. So she shouted one more time as loudly as she could with her mouth right next to a tiny gap where the fur met the stone lintel. And then she heard something, a sort of moan, as if someone were in pain. There it was again – a deep, suffering groan. It must be Corann. He sounded as if he needed help. Surely she would be forgiven for entering the temple in an emergency such as this.

Quickly, she pulled the curtain back and stepped once more across a sacred threshold.

14

T H E bearskin rug fell back across the entrance leaving Boudica in total darkness. Her eyes widened automatically, hunting for any texture in the gloom. Almost by instinct she could tell she was in a long, narrow passageway just wide enough for a man. Her eyes and hands built up a picture in the blackness. The wall was lined with cool metallic discs, possibly shields, and she was now certain she could see the faint glow of a lamp ahead. She tapped her foot on the floor. It was smooth stone. Slowly she moved forward, deeper and deeper into the temple. It was so unlike any other building Boudica had ever been in that she found it hard to believe that she was still in Sinovix. To calm her nerves she counted her steps: ten, now twenty. The light was getting brighter. Behind the discs she could see skulls with chalky teeth grimacing at her, the fallen enemy warriors of long forgotten wars. Uneasily, she hurried forward listening out for another groan, but there was nothing. She bumped into a wall. She hadn't been concentrating. The light was now coming from her right. She turned a corner and ahead of her was a large chamber. The floor had been dug out so that it was unusually high with mud walls to half its height. It was dank and cold and Boudica, who was wearing only a thin summer shift, shivered.

The light that she had seen came from a beeswax lamp burning on a large, rectangular rock in the centre of the room. The lamp was between two cauldrons, one silver, the other bronze. Apart from that, the large chamber was empty. Boudica didn't know what she had been expecting but it wasn't this vast, damp, bleak space.

It was clear that Corann was not in the room, but the force that had lured her down the dark passageway seemed to draw her to the altar. Tentatively she climbed down the steep steps. The surface of the rock was smooth and flat and granite-grey, except the centre which was stained red-brown with blood. After a sacrifice Corann carried the animal away into the temple and now she knew where they ended up. The brown patch looked sticky and several flies were hovering over it. They flew up as she approached. Cow's blood? Goat's? She didn't know, but it must be recent as it was still moist. She backed off, repulsed, and then, with a tiny splash, a droplet fell from somewhere above. Quickly she looked up. Twelve feet or more above the altar was a board made from three planks of wood held in place by a metal chain which disappeared up to the ceiling of the chamber. Whatever was on that board was still fresh enough to be dripping.

Another tiny splash of blood brought Boudica to her senses. She had seen more than enough. What was she doing here? Corann was nowhere to be found and the moaning had stopped. It must have been the wind. Suddenly she had an overwhelming desire to get out. She retraced her steps, her heart racing. She had a sudden dreadful conviction that there was no longer just the passage and the bearskin rug between her and home. There was the insurmountable task of getting out of this forbidden place. Why couldn't she have learned her lesson in the forest? She had affronted the gods with this second transgression and they were punishing her once more.

In her panic Boudica was breathing in shallow gasps which made her feel faint. Calm down, she told herself, it's not far to the bearskin. She climbed the stairs; only the passageway to go now. At the top she glanced back. Her eyes were level with the wooden board hanging over the altar. In a moment of horror she saw that dangling over the stone, was not the body of an animal but the body of a man, the very man she'd been looking for. Corann was lying there with an axe in his skull.

15

BOUDICA stood transfixed by the sight of Druid Corann with blood dripping from the hideous gash in his head. His pallid, grey skin told her he was dead. Nobody could survive such an injury. As she stared at the body, she realized with horror that she must have heard his last gasps of life. Less than an hour ago she had seen him cross the town square, humming as he went, and yet here he was, murdered. A sickening feeling came over her as she saw that the axe rooted in his skull had a wooden handle, intricately carved with a pattern of ivy leaves. It looked exactly like one belonging to her father. But her father would never do such a thing. What could possibly be going on?

Quickly she climbed the last step and turned back into the passage. And there, in front of her, was the silhouette of a tall man. It was so unexpected that she walked straight into him.

"Looking for someone?" said Bodvoc.

Boudica's mouth was so dry that she couldn't answer.

"What are you doing here?"

His voice was harsh and pressing.

Words now tumbled out of Boudica.

"I wanted Corann. Chiomara's father is ill. She thinks

he has the swelling sickness. I came here to find Corann because if anyone can cure him, he can. I knew that I shouldn't have, but it was so urgent that I couldn't wait."

"And you found him, didn't you? Let's go and see him."

Boudica felt Bodvoc's hand push her firmly back towards the chamber. Panic rose in her. She couldn't go back. She couldn't see that awful sight again.

"It's forbidden for me to enter," she said desperately.

"A bit late for that, wouldn't you say?"

Boudica could feel his steady, penetrating eyes on her. She didn't answer.

"Anyway," continued Bodvoc, "a druid may authorize anyone to enter the temple."

His hand gripped her shoulder tightly, forcing her back into the chamber. Boudica realized that begging, crying or imploring him to be merciful would make no difference, so she steeled herself as best she could. Averting her eyes from the dripping body she climbed down the stairs with Bodvoc following closely behind her.

"Cross to the altar," he commanded.

When she was standing next to it he yanked her hand up and put it on the cauldron made from beaten silver just to the left of the sticky brown patch of congealing blood.

"Boudica, you have to learn not to meddle with things you don't understand."

Boudica nodded her head in terror.

"Of course," she mumbled.

"You have seen things this afternoon that you should not have seen."

"I know. I'm sorry. I'm really, really sorry."

"Do you know what this is?"

Bodvoc pointed to the cauldron that he had her hand pressed against.

"No."

"It's a sacred bowl which has been in the possession of the Iceni for over a hundred years. Any oath taken when touching it must be kept or a terrible price will be extracted by the gods not only on the transgressor but also on their family. That means not only you but also your mother, father and sister. Do you understand?"

Bewildered, Boudica nodded.

"I want you to swear never to tell anyone what you have witnessed."

Hope. There was hope. Why would Bodvoc make her promise such a thing unless he was going to let her go? Boudica readily agreed.

"Of course, I'll do whatever you want."

"Then repeat after me, 'I vow that I will never speak to anyone of anything I have seen inside the temple this afternoon.'"

As Boudica uttered the words Bodvoc pressed her hand so hard against the cauldron that a sharp edge split the skin at the tip of her finger, drawing blood.

"That cut is a sign that the gods have heard," said the

druid with satisfaction.

Boudica looked at the crimson streak and knew that this was an oath she could never break. Bodvoc had tied her tongue for ever.

"Now get out," he said, pushing her back towards the stairs. "You'll find the medicine Belos needs outside your house later today."

Boudica was even more confused. Bodvoc could hardly know Belos. What interest could he possibly have in his illness?

"Get out, I said."

She did not have to be told a third time. She picked up her skirt and ran as fast as she could.

16

BOUDICA stumbled out into the temple courtyard, scrunching up her green eyes against the bright sunlight, and fell to her knees feeling queasy. Corann had been murdered with her father's axe. She had seen it and she could say nothing. But surely Jodoc would not be held responsible. King Antedios would know that her father was innocent. Anyone could have taken the axe from the hook where it hung in their home.

The cow in the corner pen mooed mournfully and it brought Boudica to her senses. She had to get home. This was the last place she should be seen hanging around.

Boudica was helping Tessa weave a rug when she heard the yell that she had been expecting all afternoon.

"Murder! There's been a murder!"

Dagma dropped her mending.

"Did you hear that? It sounded like 'murder'! I'll find out what's happening. You get on with your chores."

Boudica and Tessa sat on the earth floor half-heartedly plaiting dried reeds and listening to people scurrying around outside as they passed on the news.

Suddenly Tessa threw down her work and went to the door.

"Everyone's at the temple gates. How can you bear to just sit there? It's so unlike you."

This jolted Boudica. It was true that normally it would be her peeking out of the door and trying to persuade her sister to come and look. She had to be more like her usual self or Tessa might start wondering.

"Everyone's there," said Tessa. "There's really no need for us to stay here. Mother will understand."

Reluctantly Boudica followed her sister. King Antedios was walking grimly towards the temple gates, accompanied by several warriors including Jodoc. Her father was discussing something with Prince Prasutagus who was rubbing the long scar on his forehead distractedly. Both men looked worried.

"A meeting is called," shouted one of the warriors. "The king will find the culprit while the evidence is still fresh."

Boudica was swept up with all the Iceni pouring into the temple courtyard. Now that it was overflowing with people it felt like a different place from the oddly silent square she had entered that morning.

"Be seated!" King Antedios commanded.

Wherever they were, people sat on the dried mud. For once, warriors, farmers, carpenters, herdsmen and servants were all mixed up.

"Today, a terrible event has taken place," the king's

quavering voice rang out across the square. "Bodvoc has found our druid, Corann, murdered in his own temple."

A murmur of dismay echoed around the courtyard. Nobody wanted to hear the rumour confirmed.

"It appears that he was killed by a single blow of an axe. When Bodvoc found him he was lifeless but still bleeding, so it must have happened very recently. Prasutagus, have the body brought out, so that everyone may see it."

The tall prince pointed at three burly men and together they disappeared into the temple. Moments later the group emerged carrying the board with Corann's body on it and gently set down their grisly load.

"I know that axe," shouted someone in the front row. "It belongs to Jodoc."

The old king nodded wearily as if he had been expecting this. "We can all see that there has been some crude attempt to implicate Jodoc, but remember, he is one of our most trusted warriors. Just because the axe belongs to Jodoc does not mean he is the man that wielded it."

Boudica was comforted by the whisperings around her.

"The king's right enough on that."

"Would any man be fool enough to murder another with his own weapon?"

"I want to know who the real culprit is," continued the king. "Did any of you see someone go into the temple this morning? Think everyone. This is important."

Suddenly it occurred to Boudica that she could be caught in a terrible trap. If anyone had seen her what would her promise allow her to say?

A stooped old man stood up. Boudica frantically cast her mind back to the moment when she had slipped into the temple. Surely the square had been empty. She certainly remembered taking a moment to check.

"I saw Jubbah herd a cow in there just after dawn this morning," said the peasant.

Boudica sighed with relief.

"Thank you, Cannen, but Corann was seen coming back from the forest some time after that. He spoke to quite a few people on his return journey, as was his way. Anybody else?"

There was an uncomfortable silence. Boudica kept thinking: *What about Bodvoc?* Bodvoc was obviously there. Wasn't he a suspect? After all he was the one with a motive. With Corann out of the way he could become the chief druid.

Haltingly, another hand went up.

"Yes, Rhiannon," said King Antedios encouragingly.

It was one of the serving girls from the king's household. She couldn't have been much older than Tessa.

"Sire, I saw Agron go in with another man," she pointed over at the warrior, her voice wavering as she went on. "He was with the man that's sitting next to him now. Fhina is his name. It was after I had eaten my lunch. I was going to the field to fetch some parsley for tonight's meal and I saw them. They left the gate open when they went in."

"After lunch you say?"

"Yes," said the girl, becoming more confident. "Quite a bit after as I had already cleared the bowls and washed them too."

The king nodded.

"Thank you, Rhiannon, but I believe that must have been after the time of the murder. Bodvoc brought us the news during lunch. Has anyone else anything to say?"

An old farmer, without a tooth in his mouth, got to his feet. It was the man Rhiannon had pointed out.

"Yes, Fhina?"

"When we was in that temple, Agron found something. He ought to tell you about it."

"Well?" said King Antedios.

Agron stood up slowly. He seemed reluctant to get involved.

"It's nothing, sire. I'm sure it's a coincidence," he said.

"Get on with it," said the king, exasperation creeping into his voice. "What is Fhina talking about?"

"As soon as I heard the news I went to see the scene for myself," said Agron hesitantly, twisting his hands together as he spoke, as if the words were being wrung out of him. "A man can't kill another and winch him up above the altar single-handedly without leaving a trace of his presence. As I went I thought *it can't be Jodoc* and I still believe that."

"Tell him what you found," prompted Fhina, with a gummy grin. He was clearly enjoying being the centre of attention.

"Behind the altar, I found this, half trodden into the mud floor."

In his hand he held up a miniature, bronze dagger.

Fhina couldn't contain himself any more.

"Soon as I saw it I knew it wasn't from these parts and then Agron said he'd seen it before. He said when he visited Boudica, when she had that broken ankle, she'd shown it to him and she'd told him that her father takes it with him wherever he goes. So there," he finished with a flourish as if the mystery were solved.

Boudica couldn't believe what she was hearing. Her father would never do such a thing. King Antedios must know that. But now the whisperings around her were of no comfort at all.

"The axe and then a dagger, that doesn't look so clever."

"Maybe he lost his rag over something. I've seen him when he's lost his temper and he can be brutal."

Boudica's head was spinning – this couldn't be happening, this couldn't be right. Then she heard her name called.

"Boudica, come here and see if you can identify the

knife," said the king with a new harshness in his voice. "It seems it may be important."

17

BOUDICA walked slowly through the crowds to where the king was standing. Antedios held the tiny dagger in his open palm. As soon as she got within ten feet of him she could see it was the dagger that Culann had made for her.

"Child, can you identify this?" asked the king sternly.

Boudica sought out her father in the crowd, not knowing what to say.

Jodoc nodded solemnly at her, silently instructing her to tell the truth.

"Yes."

"Is it the knife that you gave to your father?"

"Yes."

"And did you tell Agron that he took it everywhere?"

Boudica was horrified. Those were exactly the words she had used, but now they seemed so incriminating. Frantically she tried to help.

"I did say that, but it doesn't mean he might not have lost it or left it behind..."

"Thank you, child," said the king. "Sit down."

Antedios looked at Jodoc with pursed lips.

"All the evidence leads back to you. Do you have

anything to say that can shed any light on this unhappy event?"

Jodoc shook his head. He looked wretched and confused. Her father was a warrior, a strong decisive man of action and it shocked Boudica to see his spirit breaking.

"You have nothing to say?" asked the king incredulously.

"I can only tell you the truth," answered Jodoc in a faltering voice. "I have not been to the temple since the festival of Beltaine and I would never hurt Druid Corann. He was my friend."

"So where did you spend the morning?" pressed the king.

"Walking in the woods, preparing for our lunch together. I knew we had many things to discuss and I wanted to think about them."

The tribe didn't like that answer, but Boudica knew her father and his ways. He often wandered in the forests as he worried his way through a problem.

"Did anyone see Jodoc?" asked the king.

There was a terrible silence.

"Jodoc, I must reflect on what your punishment will be."

"Father, aren't you being too hasty?" It was Prince Prasutagus who dared to question the king. "Jodoc is one of our finest warriors. He's served you loyally for many years. There must be another explanation..."

Boudica prayed the king would listen to his son, but the old man's face was stony.

"Prasutagus, I have made my decision. Do not question it."

"The king's right. Jodoc should be sacrificed," called a man from the back.

"Yesterday, I received an urgent message," announced Antedios curtly. "Along with ten other tribal kings, I have been summoned to Camulodunon by the Roman invader, Emperor Claudius. I leave this evening. Jodoc will be dealt with according to our customs on my return. Until then he will be locked up. Prasutagus, you will see to it."

"Where do you wish me to put him?" asked the prince.

"In a grain pit."

The king walked back through the crowd and out of the temple. Jodoc followed. His hands were tied tightly in front of him with a leather strap, and three brawny men surrounded him. Only an hour before these same men would have treated him with the respect due to a senior warrior, but now he was their prisoner.

Seeing her father being led away like an animal, Boudica was suddenly outraged by the injustice of it all. A grain pit was little more than a damp hole in the ground and a man kept in one for any length of time would go out of his mind. As Jodoc shuffled past she shouted out, "Father, it'll be all right. We'll get you out."

At once she was roughly pushed aside by one of the

guards and she fell, hitting her head on the corner of a gatepost. The pain made her dizzy; she clung to the wooden post to keep her balance as the courtyard gradually emptied. On the far side of the temple Boudica saw her mother sink to her knees, sobbing, her head in her hands. Tessa was comforting her. As soon as she felt steady enough, Boudica went over to them.

"Mother, you heard what Prince Prasutagus said. This is a mistake."

"A mistake?" said Dagma angrily, wiping her face with the back of her hand. "Don't you see? You've just condemned your own father and all for the sake of some stupid trinket."

"But what was I supposed to say?" asked Boudica, stunned by her mother's fury.

"Anything other than the answer you gave. You're responsible for this. You've as good as killed him. Get away from me."

Boudica felt her blood boiling over. The fall of Jodoc was terrible for the family. She knew it would be particularly hard on Dagma. As the wife of a traitor she would be shunned, but she was not the only one who would suffer. What about Tessa? What about Boudica? And why did Dagma always blame her for everything? It wasn't fair. She had had enough. Her mother had told her to go. Well, that's what she would do and then her mother would be sorry.

18

BOUDICA stormed out of the temple. Tessa ran after her, protesting that Dagma didn't mean what she'd said but Boudica knew better. At the moment when she'd blamed her daughter for Jodoc's predicament and told her to go away, her mother had meant every word of it.

"I'm not coming back until Mother apologizes," she said.

"But you know she won't do that. If you leave you're being just as unreasonable as she is."

Boudica shook her head.

"I don't care."

She walked quickly home and packed a small bundle of clothing. But as her hands did the things that she needed to do her mind was frozen. She knew that she had to leave but she had no idea where she was going. The only thing she was certain of was that she must get out of Sinovix.

"Come on, Cinnia."

As she left, she noticed a small clay pot just outside the door and realized it must be the medicine that Bodvoc had promised. She'd been so distracted that Belos's sickness had slipped her mind. She picked up the jar and saw that it was full of a green glutinous liquid speckled with grated bark. At least that settled the problem of where to go next. She would deliver the precious liquid to Chiomara.

In less than half an hour Boudica was at the farm watching Chiomara gently lift Belos's head, and coax him into swallowing the cloying medicine. Belos's eyes were staring ahead into the distance, looking but not seeing, and his hair was damp with sweat.

"Thank you," said Chiomara. "How did you get it so quickly?"

Briefly Boudica told her everything that had happened: Corann's murder; the finding of the dagger; Jodoc's imprisonment and her mother's reaction. The only part she left out was the bit she was forbidden to tell.

"Your mother will calm down, don't worry. She doesn't really mean it."

Boudica shook her head.

"I don't care," she answered firmly. "I'm not going back."

"Then stay here until you both come to your senses. I can't do all the work by myself with father being ill. It would be a godsend."

"Are you sure?" said Boudica. She felt giddy with relief. Not only could she stay but she was needed.

"Of course, and when I get a chance I'll tell Tessa where you are. She can let your mother know when the time is right."

Boudica was pulling up a bucket of water from the well

when Cinnia began barking.

"What is it?" she asked absent-mindedly, glancing over the fields. An evening mist had settled in the dips in the land but through the haze she could see horses galloping towards Sinovix. Her heart began to race. It must the king, returning from his visit to Emperor Claudius. He had been away for over a month. Now that he was back, Jodoc's fate would be determined.

Boudica dropped the bucket and ran back to the house.

"Chiomara, I've got to go. King Antedios is back."

So far Boudica had managed to stay away from the town entirely. It hadn't been difficult. Chiomara had been busy nursing her father back to health and the farming and all the chores had fallen to Boudica. From the fields she could see Sinovix's high wooden fence but not once had she crossed the drawbridge. Today would be different.

"I'll come with you," said Chiomara and together they picked up their skirts and ran as fast as they could.

A crowd had gathered to welcome the king. Boudica spotted her mother on the far side of the square. Their eyes locked for a moment then both of them stubbornly turned away. Neither was ready to compromise.

The crowd waited patiently for the king to report news of his journey. At last, Antedios emerged from his palace on the arm of Prince Prasutagus and climbed onto a large log in the centre of the square.

"Tribesmen, it is with a heavy heart that I must

report that the great town of Camulodunon has been destroyed. In its place over five thousand Romans and many more of their slaves are building a fort. When I saw this mighty army with my own eyes I knew that the gods had advised us well – this is an enemy that is too strong for us to defeat. However, eleven tribes, including the Iceni, the Regni, the Atrebates and the Brigantes, reached an agreement with the emperor Claudius. In return for an annual payment of one quarter of our crops and free passage to our ports they will leave us in peace and will allow us to bear arms."

There was a murmur of dissatisfaction.

"If I had not agreed to their terms," said the king sharply, "we would be Roman slaves. There must be no talk of rebellion and no one will venture onto their soil. I forbid it. From now on we will live in peace with our Roman neighbours. Any dissent will be severely punished."

"What about Jodoc?" called out a woman. "What are you going to do to him?"

"I have not forgotten that ugly business," the king answered. "As a sign of good faith the Romans have demanded a warrior from each village be sent to their army in Camulodunon. Jodoc will be sent from Sinovix. That will be his punishment."

Boudica couldn't believe her ears. Her father wouldn't be killed after all. She felt as if a great burden was lifted from her.

She turned to Chiomara.

"Did you hear that? Father's to be spared."

But her joy was short lived for a man, standing just in front of her, turned round and said with a sneer in his voice, "I don't know what you're so pleased about. It's a death sentence by another name."

19

IT was only by chance that Boudica was able to say goodbye to her father. She was working in the fields when she heard the sound of horses on the move. It was Jodoc being taken away from Sinovix by a band of Icenian warriors. Boudica recognized Kelpa's silhouette first. The proud stallion was a head taller than the accompanying horses.

As soon as she saw them Boudica ran towards the bridle path.

"Father, it's me," she called out as the horses approached.

Living in an underground pit for over a month, never seeing the sun, and being passed food through a slit in the roof had taken a terrible toll on Jodoc. His body was shrunken, his skin grey, and his head bounced limply as Kelpa trotted. It took Boudica a moment to believe that this really was her father. She began running beside him calling out, "It's Boudica," again and again over the thundering of the horses' hooves.

The Icenian warriors didn't bother to shoo her away. They knew that she couldn't keep up with them for long but thankfully Jodoc looked up. He was trying to say something to her but it was impossible to hear over the noise of the horses.

"What did you say?" Boudica called desperately but the riders were pulling away from her. There was no chance of her catching up however hard she tried but she wouldn't give in. Her side ached from the effort but still she ran on after them.

The lead warrior, Prince Prasutagus, dressed in a billowing purple cape, slowed down a little to let the rest of the group overtake him. With a last desperate spurt Boudica caught up with him.

"Please, sir, tell me, what did he say?" she begged.

"He said 'Remember you're from the Iceni.'"

The prince spoke gently and compassionately. It comforted Boudica a little.

"Tell him, I will," she said. "Tell him one day the Iceni will be proud of me."

That evening she sat outside Belos's home, waiting for the warriors to return. The Iceni and their southern neighbours, the Trinovantes, had had good relations before the Roman invasion, and her father had made frequent visits to their capital, Camulodunon. Boudica loved long rides and a couple of times Jodoc had taken her with him so she knew it was a full day's riding there and back.

At last, as the sun was setting, she saw them. Bitterly she counted the riders. Twelve men had left Sinovix and only eleven were returning. As she watched, one man broke away. Prince Prasutagus came towards her leading a beautiful black horse.

"Your father asked me to give you this stallion. The Romans were entitled to Jodoc, not his horse."

"Are you sure he wanted *me* to have him?" asked Boudica.

"Yes. He asked me to tell you that he always meant you to have Kelpa."

Prasutagus handed Boudica the leather harness.

"I think it was his way of saying he doesn't blame you for what happened."

Boudica couldn't speak. She pulled Kelpa close and buried her face in the horse's silky flank.

20

BOUDICA had been staying on the farm for six months. Chiomara couldn't have been more welcoming and to repay her kindness Boudica worked as hard as she could. Belos, who was almost back to full health, often tried to persuade her to rest but she always found that there was something more to do: water to fetch; cows to be fed; and stalls to be cleaned. The endless work was calming and stopped her thinking too much about the row with her mother and what was happening to her lost-looking father. She couldn't bear to dwell on the fact that he was somewhere alien, beyond the fens and forests, and that she had no idea what was happening to him. It was less painful to work until she was exhausted and flop into bed each night, too tired even to think.

Now the days were cold and damp and the daylight hours were few. The winter solstice, the shortest day of the year, was rapidly approaching.

"I've heard Druid Bodvoc will be leading the celebrations this year," said Chiomara one day when they were pulling up barley stubble. It was tough work. A sharp stalk cut Boudica's finger and she sucked it thoughtfully.

"Will Belos want to go?"

"Of course, now he's well enough. I think he'll expect you to come too. You know how important these ceremonies are to him."

But as soon as Boudica heard the name "Bodvoc" she knew she couldn't possibly go. Every time she thought of him she was reminded of that dreadful sight in the temple and the oath he had extracted from her. Being in the same place as him would be intolerable and on top of that her mother was bound to be there. She hadn't seen Dagma since her father had been sentenced by the king. Occasionally Tessa would visit, trying in vain to make peace between Boudica and their mother. The news she brought from home was not good. Agron had broken off their engagement saying he had no wish to be associated with a family of traitors and Dagma was taking the family's fall from grace badly. Boudica knew that it must be hard on her sister but each time she thought about returning she always came back to the same stumbling block: her mother must apologize to her first. Only then would she go home.

"This feud will go on for ever," Tessa had said in frustration last time she'd visited the farm. "You're both as bad as each other. The solstice is the time for making a fresh start. We should all be together, not arguing like this. If Father knew what was going on he'd be horrified."

Her words had set Boudica thinking and when she heard Chiomara's news about Bodvoc she made up her mind.

"Can I ask you something?"

Chiomara looked up. Something in Boudica's tone told her this was important.

"Of course, what is it?"

"I need your help. I'm going to spend this winter solstice with Father. I don't want him to be alone, but no one must know."

Boudica didn't have to explain why. King Antedios had expressly forbidden any contact with the Romans. The Iceni would only remain free as long as they paid the Romans their annual tribute and stayed off their land.

"How will you get there?" asked Chiomara.

"I have Kelpa. He can easily do the ride in a day. That's not the hard part. The hard part is not getting found out. If I pretend to be sick that morning, could you convince Belos that I'm too ill to come to the temple, but not ill enough to worry about? I'll leave straight after you've gone and be back before you return. You're bound to be very late."

"Why don't you let me come too?"

"No," said Boudica. "It's dangerous. I'll be safer alone."

Boudica held on tight to Kelpa's reins as she raced across the open countryside. Chiomara had played her part perfectly and she had twelve precious hours to get to Camulodunon and back.

Snow had fallen heavily over the previous two days.

She'd been worried about whether it would still be possible to make the journey, but that morning she'd woken to a brilliant blue sky.

After many hours in the saddle, trekking south across the fens, her legs and back were beginning to ache. The late afternoon air was still and cold, freezing her hands. She clasped a white wolfskin cape round her and bound her hands in strips of cloth but the biting wind always seemed to find a way through.

The grey afternoon light turned to dusk but the sky was clear and soon a bright, full moon illuminated the path for her. Although the trail was pockmarked with hooves she hadn't seen another rider. Tribes all over Britain would be busy celebrating the solstice tonight.

The path left the wetland and led into the forests, marking the beginning of Trinovantian territory, except that it was now Roman land. Boudica knew that Camulodunon was close.

In no time she was through the woods and looking down a broad valley. At its base was the silvery ribbon of a river and next to it a patch of light that marked the city. But the patch of light was all wrong. Boudica searched for familiar landmarks – the central round house, the sacred temple, the drawbridge – but they weren't there. The capital of the Trinovantes had been wiped from the earth and in its place was a new town nothing like the one that had been there before.

It was made up of over twenty rectangular buildings

placed at regular intervals round a central square. Celtic villages had round houses, some large, some small, scattered within the village walls, and even tumbling outside where space was tight. The geometric regulation unnerved Boudica – people that built like this must be different.

The camp was built within a stone wall with a central wooden gate. Even from this distance she could see that the wall was too high to climb. She'd have to find another way in if she was going to see her father. Her eyes followed the wall and she saw that on the far side, it dipped out of view. She looked more closely. Perhaps it wasn't finished yet. That was the place to start, but between her and this gap was a wide grey gash in the snowy landscape, as if the gods had reached down and cut the ground. It must be a path of some kind.

Boudica steered Kelpa into the woods where there was little chance of them being seen, and tied his reins to the trunk of a birch tree. Kelpa snorted two billowing clouds of steam as if in disgust at being abandoned.

"Wait till I get back," Boudica whispered as she stroked his long nose. "I won't be too long."

She picked her way through the ferns and bracken of the thicket. Although the crisp snow only came up to her ankles, in no time her leather moccasins were cold and wet. She headed east towards the strange path but as she got closer she realized that if she were to cross it, it would be impossible to stay hidden. On either side the wood had been cleared so efficiently that not even a tree stump remained.

Boudica stared in amazement. To her left the sinister road led to the distant gates of the Roman fort. To the right it stretched away as far as the eye could see. She had never seen anything like it. The route from Sinovix to Canna was a mud track, the grass worn away by the wheels of carts and the hooves of horses, but this was completely different. This was built by man and not just one man but many thousands all working to some strange pattern. She suddenly wanted to get away from it as quickly as possible. Swiftly, she ran across the barren land, over the flat cobblestones and then into the opposite wood.

Relieved to be back in the safety of the forest Boudica worked her way towards the fort, until she saw what she had been hoping for. The wall wasn't finished – there was a gap of perhaps a hundred yards running down to the river where stone had only been laid up to three feet high. Several buckets and a large pile of rocks were lying at the base.

Boudica checked carefully around her. Every couple of hundred yards along the wall Roman soldiers were patrolling. They wore identical silver coloured metal helmets and scarlet capes, dyed a brighter red than any cloth she'd ever seen. It made them easy to spot and at this incomplete section of wall there didn't seem to be anyone very close. The white fur she was wearing was a perfect camouflage. Pulling it up tightly over her head she crawled out of the forest on her stomach. The freezing snow got into her eyes and filled her nostrils but she shuffled forward until she touched stone. Neatly, she tucked herself in under the low wall as tightly as she could and then squatted on her haunches and peered over.

Up close the camp was even more impressive. The buildings were huge. The largest had two storeys, as if built for giants, with windows and shutters and tiled roofs like overlapping shields. But the thing that surprised Boudica most was the number of men milling around all wearing those crimson capes and metal armour with oddly bare faces. Not one of them had a beard or even a moustache. In Sinovix a man would be ashamed to present such a youthful face to the world. As she examined them it dawned on her for the first time what an impossible task she had set herself. There were hundreds of men – and no women. Even if she did get inside the encampment she'd never find her father among so many and a female dressed in British clothes would be spotted immediately. It was hopeless.

Glumly she sat back down for a moment, then shook herself. *Don't give in so easily, there must be a way*, she thought. She got to her knees, looking for anything that would help, when suddenly her arms were wrenched backwards while someone else slid a hand firmly across her mouth. Gasping for breath she tried frantically to wriggle free but it was futile. She was caught; there was no escape.

21

BOUDICA kicked out hard at whoever was holding her. They were too strong for her to get away but she wouldn't be taken without a fight. The hand across her face was making it hard to breathe so she sunk her teeth into it and heard a gratifying "Ow!", but the hand only tightened.

"Shush! Do you want to get us all killed?" whispered a gruff voice.

It was the voice of a man and he was speaking her language. Maybe she'd have a chance to explain that she was the daughter of an Icenian warrior and persuade them to let her go.

The two men half carried and half dragged her back over the snowy field and into the woods. As soon as they were safely in the shadows of the trees, they dropped her on the ground like an old bearskin. Boudica lay winded, trying to get her breath back, and then, instinctively, leapt up to run. A hand grabbed her ankle.

"Hey, don't give us any more trouble."

It was a voice she recognized. "Prince Prasutagus?" He nodded grimly, sucking a bleeding finger.

"What are you doing here?" asked Boudica.

"I might well ask you the same thing. You're supposed to be at the temple."

"You too," said Boudica defiantly.

"She's got some cheek," said the other man with a flicker of amusement in his eyes.

"We spotted you crossing the road," said Prasutagus. "Do you know that if the Romans had found you, you would have been killed?"

"I was careful," said Boudica.

Prasutagus shook his head in dismay. The girl was showing no gratitude at all and he'd just risked his life for her.

"You still haven't answered my question."

"I wanted to see my father. He's a conscript in their army," she explained for the stranger's benefit.

"Not in the army," said the stranger. "They're all either Romans or foreigners. If he's a Briton and he's here then he must be one of their slaves."

Boudica felt as if she'd been punched in the stomach. Her father, an Icenian warrior, a slave! There would be more honour in death. Then her distress turned to fury. She knew whose fault this was – the man she had disliked from the first moment she saw him, the man who must have seen Corann's murderer but, for some reason, wouldn't say.

"Bodvoc's to blame," she said vehemently.

"Druid Bodvoc?" The stranger looked perplexed.

"Yes."

"He can't be. He's on our side."

"No he's not," said Boudica.

"Be careful how you address this man," warned Prasutagus. "This is King Caradoc, the only warrior with the courage to save Britain from Rome."

For once, Boudica was stunned into silence. This was the man who was supposed to be organizing a rebellion against the Romans. Caradoc was wiry, shorter than Prasutagus and a generation older, with the fair colouring of the southern tribes. He didn't look anything like a king or a hero, but he was both.

"You should trust Bodvoc," said Caradoc. "He's a good man."

"I'm afraid I know better, sir," said Boudica, much more politely now.

"And how is that?"

"I can't say."

"Then I can't refute it, but you should believe me as I know the man well."

Boudica didn't answer. Nothing anybody said could make her change her mind about Bodvoc.

"Sir, I know you have to leave soon," interrupted Prasutagus. "Tell me what you need to know."

At once Caradoc rattled off a series of questions. How many legionnaires, centurions and auxiliaries were there at Camulodunon? Five thousand men in a unit they call the Twentieth Legion, answered Prasutagus. How many chariots did they have? Perhaps two hundred. Did Prasutagus yet know the pattern of their patrols? Not fully. How much grain did they have in store? Enough for at least one winter.

Boudica listened carefully. There was a ruthless intensity to Caradoc's questions. It was clear that he wanted to know about every aspect of Roman life and that Prasutagus knew most of the answers. To have so much information the prince must have been coming here night after night, despite the warnings of King Antedios.

At last the men were finished.

"Where are you going now?" asked Prasutagus.

"West to the Silures. They'll be my base from now on. I need to get more tribes on our side before we are ready to take on the Romans. There's no chance of changing your father's mind, is there?"

"I'll do what I can," said Prasutagus, "but right now he's convinced that we should stay out of it."

Caradoc nodded grimly.

"I thought so. If you get more useful information then pass it on through the druids. They can always be trusted and it takes surprisingly little time to reach me."

Caradoc picked up a satchel and then turned to Boudica.

"I can see that you are tough and brave. One day we'll need Britons like you."

Boudica glowed with pride.

"There goes the finest Briton I've ever met," said

Prasutagus as Caradoc disappeared into the forest. "He almost defeated the Romans at Medway and he won't give up. He's dedicated his life to expelling them from our country. You should be honoured to have met him."

"I am," Boudica answered truthfully. "I really am."

Here, at last, was a man that might help free her father, and she would do anything she could to help him.

22

AS they rode back along the bridle path to Sinovix, Boudica asked Prasutagus how often he came to spy on Camulodunon.

"Ever since the Romans conquered it, I've come when I can," he replied. "I saw them destroy the old town. They burned everything – homes, animals and wheat – and then they built that fort you saw. It's amazing the effort they've gone to. It's got barracks, stores, a temple, even a place to wash, and do you know why?"

Boudica was a little frightened by his grim tone. She shook her head.

"Because they're planning to stay for ever."

As he spoke Prasutagus clenched his fist.

"Well at least they're keeping out of Icenian territory," said Boudica.

"For now."

"You think they'll come north?"

"North, south, east and west unless we're ready for them. King Caradoc is the key. He's prepared to put up a fight."

"Does King Antedios know what you're doing?" asked Boudica tentatively.

"No, and he mustn't." Prasutagus looked at Boudica with his steely blue eyes.

"Of course."

She had answered his unspoken question. He could trust her. She had more reason to hate the Romans than almost any other Iceni: her father was one of their slaves. The sooner King Caradoc, or anybody else, could lead a rebellion and free him, the better.

They rode on through the night. The wind had now picked up and the snow was drifting. Boudica's hands were freezing and the end of her nose had lost all feeling. The moon was high in the sky when they came at last into their valley.

"You know your way from here?" asked Prasutagus.

"Yes, of course," said Boudica and then on the spur of the moment she added, "If you ever see my father, please tell me how he is."

"It won't be good," said Prasutagus gently. "Slaves built that road and the fort. They work in freezing weather for hour after hour. No man can endure it for long."

Boudica understood what Prasutagus was trying to tell her, but she needed to know, however bad the news was.

"Anything you find out, you can tell me."

The fields of wheat and spelt that Boudica had helped Chiomara and Belos plant had grown to waist height.

"Not long now," said Belos, running a hand along the

wheat ears. "As long as we don't get any rain, it'll be a good harvest."

"Boudica," said Chiomara, "let's sit under the trees for a while. We've been working all day. There's really nothing left to do."

The leaves in the forest glowed every shade of green in the afternoon sun. They settled down on either side of a birch tree and rested against the trunk, each lost in thought. A bee droned and in the distance the crazed knocking of a woodpecker could be heard. It made Boudica feel sleepy. Her heavy eyelids slipped shut.

"Wake up, it's me."

It took her a moment to focus.

"Prince Prasutagus?"

The young man nodded solemnly. It was the first time she'd seen him since that night at the Roman fort. He must have news for her.

"You've seen my father, haven't you?"

The prince rubbed his scar distractedly. It was the gesture of a man not quite sure how to say what he had to say.

"Where is he?"

"Where no one can hurt him. He's free at last."

"What are you talking about?" said Boudica, even though in her heart she knew.

"Jodoc's dead. The work killed him."

Boudica let out an anguished sob and her cry woke Chiomara.

"What's wrong?" she demanded, hurrying from behind the tree.

Prasutagus looked startled.

"Don't worry, she's my best friend," said Boudica, and she told Chiomara the dreadful news.

"Where's the body?" asked the practical Chiomara. "He must have a decent funeral."

"I brought it with me," said the prince grimly. "It's waiting for you deeper in the forest but we must be quick."

Prasutagus led them to a clearing and Boudica approached her father slowly. She was scared of what she would see, but she needn't have worried. Jodoc looked as if he had fallen asleep on one of his walks. It was strangely comforting.

"I found this in his pocket," said Prasutagus. "It will serve as the offering."

He handed Boudica the miniature dagger that Culann had made all those months ago. Boudica threw it down – the knife had got her father into so much trouble and she never wanted to see it again.

"It's a message from your father," said Chiomara. "He kept it because you gave it to him. It's the perfect offering." She picked the knife up from the forest floor. "Be happy that Prince Prasutagus was kind enough to bring him to you."

Boudica came to her senses.

"I'm sorry, I wasn't thinking." She turned to Prasutagus. "How can I ever repay you?"

He patted her shoulder reassuringly.

"You're not the only person who admired and respected your father. We'll do right by him."

"Thank you. I must tell them at home," said Boudica. This was the time for reconciliation. The stupid quarrel with her mother must not go on a moment longer or what was left of her family would be permanently torn apart.

"You can't," said Prasutagus firmly. "You must bury him alone, here."

"Why?"

"Because otherwise you'll have to explain how the body got back. Don't you see, if you do that you'll be putting me and King Caradoc and maybe the whole rebellion at risk."

Boudica realized she was trapped. She couldn't betray the rebellion or her father's death might never be avenged, but she decided that she would be reconciled with her mother as soon as she got the chance.

"Shall we build the pyre here?" she asked.

"No," said Prasutagus. "We can't do that either – the smoke would be seen. We must bury him the way our ancestors did."

He was right, but Boudica felt she must make preparations for her father's journey to the other world. He would need food, drink and some bowls at the very least.

"Do I have time to fetch a leg of pork and some mead from the farm?" she asked.

"Yes, while I finish off the grave." Prasutagus pointed to a deep pit on the far side of the clearing.

Boudica and Chiomara ran as fast as they could and were soon back carrying a small bundle. Together they lined the pit with oak leaves, rowan branches and mistletoe from the forest and then Prasutagus carefully laid the corpse in it. Boudica passed down the meat, a bottle of mead and two clay plates. It wasn't much, in fact it was pitifully little. A warrior like Jodoc should have been buried with a shield, gold, swords and warm clothing, but it was something to sustain him in the other world.

The prince began covering the body with earth.

"You two go on. I'll finish here."

Boudica and Chiomara walked solemnly through the forest towards a waterfall where the river tumbled over the rocks. It was time to ask the gods to set Jodoc's spirit free. At the top of the fall, where the water rushed past, Boudica took the knife from her pocket and threw it in the pool below as her offering to the Goddess Andraste.

Chiomara took Boudica's hand.

"That was well done. Your father would have been proud."

"He'll be prouder still when I avenge his death," said Boudica resolutely, "and before Andraste, I swear one day, however long it takes, that's what I'll do."

23

"H EY! Where are you?"

Boudica and Chiomara were smearing ash onto the walls of a grain pit to keep the rats at bay. It was a messy business and they were covered with gloop from their fingertips to their elbows.

"It's Father," said Chiomara. "I wonder what's up."

Belos was a gentle, calm man who never got worked up about anything but he sounded strangely excited.

"Let's clean up and find out."

They dipped their arms into a bucket of cold water and started scrubbing, but before they could wash away all the sticky cinders Belos peered down into the hole.

"I thought I'd find you here," he said, catching his breath.

"What is it, Father?" asked Chiomara.

"I've been to Sinovix. King Antedios died in the night. Prasutagus is now king."

Chiomara and Boudica were too shocked to speak. Antedios had ruled the tribe all their lives. And he had been an old man for as long as they could remember.

"Was he ill?" asked Boudica, trying to make sense of the news.

"I don't know," said Belos, "not that I've heard, but he's

said to be over fifty. It's a great age. Anyway, he'll be cremated in four days and we must all go to the ceremony."

Chiomara and Boudica got up early on the day of the funeral. The night before, they had gone down to the stream to wash their tartan skirts and shawls. The clothes hung in front of the fire overnight, filling the roundhouse with the heavy smell of damp wool.

They walked up the valley with Belos. The town was like a spider at the centre of a web of footpaths. On every trail Icenian families from outlying farms were coming to pay their respects, for the news of Antedios's death had spread across the territory.

The temple gates had been open since dawn and by the time Boudica arrived there was standing room only.

When the courtyard was full, Bodvoc emerged from the temple followed by six Iceni carrying the king's body. They laid it on a pyre which the druid then lit with a torch. Slowly, as the crowd watched in respectful silence, the flames took hold. The only sound was the crackling and spitting of burning wood. The king's cloak was now alight. Suddenly the centre of the fire collapsed; he slipped out of view and the flames consumed him.

Prasutagus stepped forward and raised his father's shield, its cobalt engravings catching the light of the dying sun.

"You must all come to the palace and feast," shouted the young king.

"I'll see you later," said Boudica to Chiomara as the Iceni poured out of the temple and headed for the central roundhouse.

She had decided to approach her mother after the feast. Even though she could not reveal her father's death there must be a reconciliation, but the feast was not the right place. After it was over they could talk – until then she would stay out of sight.

She pushed her way across the temple bridge and walked briskly to the town's gates. Once outside, she sat down, leaning against the wooden fence.

The rolling fields of the Sinovix valley glowed in the setting sun. It was a time of day Boudica had always loved. She ran her eyes lazily over the crops rippling in the gentle breeze and then stopped as something glinting on the southern horizon caught her attention. Was it some late mourners who had only just heard of the king's death? She watched the column of people snake down into the valley, growing longer and longer. As it got closer she could see that it was a procession of horses cantering towards her. Each rider carried a spear and a rectangular shield and their tunics were red. Her blood ran cold. It was the same bright, scarlet colour she had seen the night she went looking for her father at Camulodunon. The Romans were coming to Sinovix. She had to warn the king as soon as possible.

24

"THE Romans are coming!" shouted Boudica.

Her mouth was so dry that no one heard her above the noise of the crowd heading towards the palace.

She tugged the sleeve of the nearest man. He must be from an outlying farm for she didn't recognize him.

"I've just seen the Romans. You've got to believe me. Someone must get a message to King Prasutagus."

For a moment the man looked at her as if she were mad, but her panic was hard to ignore.

"Are you sure?"

"I'm certain. They'll be here any moment. They're already in the valley."

The man turned to his friends.

"Here, this girl says Romans are coming!"

The news spread like wildfire. Several men ran to the gates to see if it was true. Mothers picked up their children, trying desperately to find a safe place to hide. Vainly, Prasutagus tried to organize his warriors.

"For god's sake, close the gates!"

But it was too late. Several hundred cavalry poured into the crowded square. The Iceni struggled to get out of the way of the wild-eyed horses. For most of them this was their first view of the feared invaders. A sullen hush fell over the tribe.

A tall man, riding the lead stallion, began barking orders in a strange language. He was dressed in a scarlet tunic and matching cape and on his head was a bronze helmet with wings, the size of a hand, on each side.

Boudica could hardly bear to look at him. He was clearly their leader so he must be responsible for what had happened to her father. His thick lips were shouting harsh, guttural words that she couldn't understand but she could tell he was brutal and cruel and that he scorned them all. Well one day, she thought grimly, he would learn that the Iceni were not to be trifled with.

The Roman general pointed to a soldier standing next to him. In a heavy accent the man translated his commands.

"Where is the man that calls himself king?"

Prasutagus stepped forward.

"I am now king of the Iceni." Boudica was impressed by how calm Prasutagus sounded. There was not a quiver of fear in his voice. "What are you doing on our land? My father, Antedios, made a treaty with you less than a year ago."

"The general will speak with you in private," said the translator. "Tell your people not to move."

Prasutagus nodded his agreement and the general

jumped from his horse and followed him to the roundhouse, with the translator trailing behind.

The people in the square remained almost silent. Only the horses snorted and pawed the ground impatiently with their sharp hooves.

The translator returned, calling out to the crowd, "Where is your druid?"

Bodvoc stepped forward.

"Bring your most sacred object here, straightaway."

Bodvoc disappeared into the temple and emerged moments later carrying a silver cauldron. Boudica realized with a shiver that it was the very one that she had taken her terrible oath on.

The translator led Bodvoc into the palace. The tribe remained quiet but curious. Had the Romans come to steal their treasures? A low hum of conversation began, but shortly afterwards the two Romans reappeared and mounted their horses. The man with the winged helmet shouted out an instruction to his men which must have been the command to leave. There was little space in the crowded square and the Romans turned their horses regardless of the chaos they caused. Everywhere people tried to dodge thundering hooves. The noise was deafening as they ran screaming wildly this way and that, and the soldiers kicked anyone who got in their way no matter how young or old. Instinctively Boudica crouched down with her head in her hands. A black horse brushed against her and she felt a sharp thump in the back which toppled her over. She was now flat on the ground with the wind knocked out of her. She rolled up into a ball. Another black stallion came galloping past, its hooves crashing either side of her head, missing her by inches.

Boudica was more frightened than she'd ever been in her life. *They're going to kill us*, she thought. *They're really going to kill us.*

She curled up in the mud trying to block out the screams around her, expecting any moment to feel the crushing weight of a horse's hoof, but gradually the noise began to subside. She looked up and saw the last horse jump carelessly over a terrified child and canter away out of the gate.

Thank goodness, they've gone, she thought.

She got to her feet unsteady, shaking and very angry. The Romans had behaved like animals, deliberately humiliating her tribe. It wasn't enough that they had conquered the southern tribes. They wanted every Briton to know that they were a power to be reckoned with. Prasutagus was right; they would spread north, south, east and west until the whole country was under their control unless something was done.

Chiomara appeared breathlessly in front of her.

"Are you all right?" she gabbled. "When I saw that horse rear over you I thought..." She couldn't complete the sentence.

Boudica spat some grit out of her mouth.

"Don't worry about me," she said. "I'm fine. It's those barbarians we must do something about."

BOUDICA marched out of the square, into the roundhouse, bursting in on Prasutagus. The room was crowded with Icenian warriors standing round the central fire and talking urgently.

"I need to speak to you," she said looking at Prasutagus with fierce, wide eyes, her wild, flaming-red hair glinting in the firelight. Her face and clothes were splattered with mud and she had a graze on her forehead.

The warriors looked askance at her. This was no way for a young girl to behave to the king.

"Have you no respect?" asked an old man at the back of the group.

Boudica was too angry to notice. There was something she had to say to the king and she needed to say it now.

She stood resolutely, hands on hips, staring at Prasutagus as if daring him to throw her out. The king capitulated. Wearily he said, "Men, give me a moment. This won't take long."

As soon as the room was cleared Boudica said, "You can't stand by and let the Romans treat us this way. They killed my father and they'll do the same to the rest of us if you give them the chance."

"Boudica, these things are complicated..." interjected Prasutagus.

"No, they're not," she said resolutely, her green eyes burning with fury. "You can do something. I know how you feel about them. Now you're king, you can order the Iceni to join with King Caradoc."

Prasutagus shook his head sadly.

"It's not as simple as that."

"Why not?" asked Boudica. "Why can't you just go out there and command every man to saddle a horse and ambush the Roman cavalry right now?"

Prasutagus looked at her steadily.

"I trusted you before, and I'll trust you again. The general delivered a message to me."

"So?" asked Boudica.

"He told me that Queen Cartimandua is holding my brother hostage. If I lift a finger against Rome she will have him killed."

It took a moment for the news to sink in. Prince Godrig, who should be returning home any day, was a captive of Cartimandua and she was using him to hold the Iceni to ransom. But Cartimandua was a Briton. It didn't make any sense. How could she betray them this way?

"Why would she do that?" asked Boudica.

"Rome has agreed to leave her kingdom alone, as long as she keeps the northern tribes in check. She's the buffer at the edge of the Roman empire."

Boudica was horrified. Cartimandua could be unreasonable, she knew that, even cruel, but this was treacherous. Prasutagus mustn't allow her to control the Iceni in this way.

"You can send a raiding party and get Prince Godrig back," protested Boudica. "He could be home within days and then you would be free to act."

"I can't," said Prasutagus. "That's why the general summoned Druid Bodvoc. He made me swear an oath on the sacred cauldron that I wouldn't try to save my brother and I wouldn't ask or allow any of my warriors to do so either."

Boudica's mind began racing. Prasutagus had promised that he wouldn't do anything and neither would any of his warriors, but that didn't include her. She could rescue Prince Godrig and free the Iceni from Cartimandua's hold. She knew the way to Canna and she was so young nobody would suspect a thing.

"I could go. The oath doesn't apply to me," she said.

"There's nothing you could do," said the king. "Even a warrior would struggle against the Brigantes and you're only a child."

"But don't you see?" said Boudica excitedly. "That's why I'm perfect. Just give me twenty days and a horse for Chiomara. That's all I'm asking."

The king looked at her steadily, rubbing his beard all the while. Boudica could feel him calculating the odds of her being successful. The tension was unbearable but, at last, he said wearily, "No, Boudica. I can't let you do this. It would be sending you to a death trap."

Boudica left as soon as she could. The king wouldn't give her his blessing, but that wasn't going to stop her. She might be the Iceni's only chance.

26

BOUDICA and Chiomara galloped hard through the marshlands. Boudica was on Kelpa and Chiomara on a chestnut mare called Cerrig which they had "borrowed" from Prasutagus's herd. They were following the bridle path that Boudica had travelled on less than a year before when she had come back from the Brigantes. She could hardly bear to think of the changes that had taken place in her life since then. Her father had been killed, the Romans had conquered much of Britain, Camulodunon had been destroyed and now Queen Cartimandua was holding the Iceni to ransom, forcing them to be Roman minions.

From the moment Boudica had made up her mind to rescue Prince Godrig she'd wanted Chiomara at her side. Chiomara was loyal, practical and brave and she'd needed little persuasion – after all she was an Iceni. They had quickly decided they must leave that day, while the town was still in disarray. Once people realized they'd gone, Boudica was sure that Prasutagus would provide Belos with an explanation. He might even speak to her mother. Boudica couldn't be certain that she would ever return from this journey and she hated the thought of their quarrel continuing. Whatever each of them had said or done it didn't matter any longer. Perhaps the king would understand that and help make it better.

The sky was dark when they reached the tower of rocks that marked the end of Icenian territory. Both girls climbed respectfully off their horses and added a stone to the mound.

"Let's pray that we can add another soon," said Boudica grimly.

"Are you sure you know the way?" asked Chiomara.

"Yes. We keep following the path that heads north of where the sun sets. That will lead us to the Brigantes."

Kelpa and Cerrig were tiring. They hadn't stopped since leaving Sinovix. Boudica spotted a clearing to her left with a stream bubbling through it.

"Let's rest here for the night," she shouted over her shoulder.

"Not too close to the path," said Chiomara. "Just in case anybody comes this way."

For the next four days they rode relentlessly, stopping only when their horses were flagging. Whenever they saw another traveller they would ride off the path into the forest; two twelve-year-olds travelling alone so far away from their tribe would be bound to invite unwelcome attention.

On the morning of the fifth day they passed the gruesome statue that marked the end of Corieltauvian territory and the beginning of the land of the Brigantes.

That afternoon Boudica spotted the ridge that dropped steeply down into the Canna valley.

"We'll hide Cerrig and Kelpa in the forest down there and wait for nightfall," she said.

27

THE crack of a twig and then a snort disturbed Boudica. She woke, sitting twelve feet above the ground on a damp branch, leaning against a knobbly tree trunk that scratched her back each time she moved. It had seemed the safest place to rest as earlier they'd spotted wolf paw prints in the mud.

Boudica reached up and shook Chiomara, who was sleeping on another branch.

"What is it?" she whispered.

"Just a boar," answered Boudica. "The horses frightened it off. But we've slept for ages. Look, the sky's pitch black. We should get going."

Boudica tried to sound as casual as she could. There was no point telling Chiomara about the butterflies fluttering around her stomach. She was probably feeling the same way and talking about it wouldn't help.

They checked Kelpa and Cerrig were firmly tied up and packed what little food they had left into a saddlebag. There was only one small joint of salted pork and three loaves of stale bread. It was not enough to get them home, but it would get them out of Brigantian territory.

"Are you ready?" asked Boudica, hoping her wavering voice didn't betray her nerves.

"I think so," said Chiomara.

"Then let's go."

Their feet crunched on stiff, frozen leaves as they crept, under cover of darkness, towards the wooden fence that surrounded the town.

There was not a breath of wind and black wood smoke rose in vertical plumes from a fire on which someone was cooking bacon. They hadn't had a decent meal for days and the delicious smell of sizzling pork fat made their stomachs ache.

"Smells good, doesn't it?" whispered Chiomara.

"Yes," said Boudica. "I'm having some as soon as we get home."

They reached the fence and peeped through a crack. Most of the houses were dark and closed up for the night but here and there little lights flickered. Canna wasn't yet quite asleep. They would have to wait a little longer.

"Follow me," mouthed Boudica.

The boar in the forest had reminded her of something that had happened when she was staying with the Brigantes: a wild pig had forced its way into the town and caused havoc, careering around, snorting and pawing the ground before charging the men that tried to corner it. If a boar could get in, they could, she thought, and she was pretty sure she knew how.

They circled the fence until they reached a place some two thirds of the way round where a large elm tree grew.

By the end of summer the great tree sucked so much moisture out of the earth that the wooden fence cracked and split and the Brigantes filled the gaps with mud.

In no time Boudica found a patched up part and they scratched away at the dried mud with their nails until they made a hole that was just big enough to squeeze through.

"I'll go first," said Boudica.

"Where will we come out?" asked Chiomara.

"Near the sheep pen, but they shouldn't make too much noise. They're used to people."

Boudica lay on her stomach and squeezed forward. After some painful wriggling, she was covered in earth and had ripped a sleeve, but she'd done it. She was in Canna.

"Your turn," she whispered.

Chiomara, who was slighter, managed to slide through more easily.

"I'm in," she said triumphantly as she got to her feet.

"And now you can get out again," said a nasal voice.

Boudica's heart sank as a tall man with lifeless eyes and sallow skin stepped out from behind an outhouse. He was dressed in the grubby robes of a shepherd but with his shock of long grey hair there was no disguising who he was. Bodvoc. She was stunned and then furious. She had always known that Bodvoc was a traitor and here was the final proof.

28

"WHAT on earth are you doing here?" Bodvoc asked them.

Boudica couldn't think of any plausible explanation so she told him the truth.

"We've come to take Prince Godrig home. Queen Cartimandua is holding him against his will."

Bodvoc looked incredulous.

"Are you telling me you two girls are a rescue party? Is that the best the Iceni can do?"

"You know there's nobody else who can come," answered Boudica, "but you wouldn't care about that. You're on their side anyway."

Bodvoc's mouth twitched with irritation.

"Of course I'm not, you stupid child."

Boudica was enraged. She'd seen with her own eyes how he'd manipulated the Iceni and only that wretched oath had stopped her from being able to warn everyone.

"Bodvoc, I know what you're up to. You haven't fooled me," she said.

"So tell me, what am I doing?"

"You're stopping us fighting the Romans. You're working for them and you're a traitor."

As she spat out the last word Bodvoc did something

unexpected: he laughed. The laugh rumbled up from deep inside him making his shoulders shake and his pale eyes water.

"What on earth are you talking about?"

"I saw you pass a message to a stranger on the other side of the sacred forest."

"I know. I tried to warn you off at the festival of Beltaine."

"And then there's that other thing – that you've forbidden me to discuss."

"I free you from your promise. You mean the murder in the temple."

"Yes. You killed Druid Corann to get control of our tribe. And you helped the Romans against Prasutagus – how convenient that you were there to administer the oath."

"Boudica, what's going on?" asked Chiomara, who'd so far been too overawed by the presence of a druid to say anything but was now too confused to stay silent. "What are you both talking about?"

Bodvoc put his hands on Boudica's shoulders. She tried to shake him away but he stopped her.

"I see I'm going to have to do some explaining. Will you at least hear me out?"

He led them to an outhouse where hay was stored for winter. The barn was almost full of rolled up bales piled one on top of the other like a giant honeycomb. They climbed up and sat in the eaves of the store.

"Boudica," Bodvoc said wearily, "I'm afraid you've misunderstood everything. If we're going to get out of here alive then we'll have to work together, so listen." He paused and then said flatly, "I came from the Isle of Mona to Sinovix because I was invited to, by Druid Corann."

"I don't believe it..." interjected Boudica.

"Hear me out. Corann sent a message through the druid network. He was concerned that there was a spy in the tribe who was giving information to the Romans and he wanted help. He didn't know who it was, so I was sent as a fresh pair of eyes and ears. Druids can go where others can't and I am a good friend of Caradoc's, so Corann knew I could be trusted."

"You know King Caradoc?"

"Yes and I understand that you're acquainted with him too."

Boudica was puzzled. She hadn't told anybody about her encounter with the rebel king. The only people who knew were Prasutagus and King Caradoc himself.

"When I came to Sinovix," Bodvoc went on, "I had no idea who I was looking for. All Corann had discovered was that a man rode to the far side of the sacred forest each new moon. It's the only place where he couldn't be seen from Sinovix and he never came into the town. As soon as I arrived, I met the traveller 'accidentally' and agreed on that day in the wood I would give him a balm for an earache he was suffering from. I thought that over time I might learn much from him but after you interrupted us he never appeared again so I never did discover why he came."

Boudica was still far from convinced.

"What about at the feast of Beltaine when the hare told us to fight the Romans? You changed the rules to stop us."

"I didn't change the rules," said Bodvoc firmly, "I interpreted them differently. But you're right; I did want to stop the Iceni from rushing into an unplanned attack. You weren't ready. Caradoc had specifically asked me to try and slow things down until all the tribes were united. He knows how skilfully the Romans use any divisions between us. The danger was that the Iceni were too far ahead of the Silures and the remnants of the Trinovantes."

Bodvoc was sounding more and more convincing but how could he explain away the worst thing of all?

"So what about the murder of Corann? Did I misunderstand that as well?" Boudica asked sarcastically.

Chiomara looked more and more surprised.

"Yes," answered Bodvoc, "it appears you did. I found Corann moments before you, but too late to see who did it. But I was certain that whoever it was would make themselves known in time. And then you came crashing in. The last thing I wanted was for the assassin to think that there might be witnesses, so I swore you to secrecy. And I was right. He gave himself away soon enough in his finding of 'evidence'."

Bodvoc said the word contemptuously.

"You mean Agron?" said Boudica. "You're mad. He was horrified when he found the dagger. You saw how he tried to clear my father. After all he was engaged to his daughter."

"No, I'm afraid he used his engagement to Tessa to get closer to Jodoc. Think about it. If Agron had found the dagger it would have been too obvious, so instead he made it look as if it were a confession being wrung out of him."

"It wasn't him," said Boudica. "I damned Father with that wretched dagger."

"No, you didn't," said Bodvoc. "You gave Agron something to plant in the temple, that's all. If it hadn't been the dagger he would have found something else. I've thought about it a hundred times and I'm certain it's so, but unfortunately I couldn't convince Antedios. He felt that the evidence against your father was too strong."

Boudica wanted to say "No, you're wrong," but just then an image came into her head of her carving the little doll and telling Agron about the origins of the knife, and she remembered the greedy look on his face. Perhaps Bodvoc was right. But why?

"He did ask me about the dagger," she said slowly. "But why would he want to kill Corann or make it look like my father did it?"

"I can't be certain, but perhaps Corann and your

father had just discovered that he was the spy."

"So *he* told the Romans about King Prasutagus's plans to join the resistance once the old king died?"

"Not the Romans, no. He told Queen Cartimandua and she passed it on."

"Are you sure?" said Boudica.

"I'm certain of it."

"How can you be?"

"Because the traitor's here right now, drinking mead with the queen. He left Sinovix shortly before you. I followed him and as soon as he was out of sight of the town he headed north. We druids have known for years that Cartimandua is not to be trusted. She's in league with the Romans and would have told them to find a way to stop Prasutagus as soon as he was crowned."

Boudica looked at Bodvoc. He was either the finest actor in the land or she had made a colossal mistake.

"I feel such an idiot," she said simply.

Bodvoc patted her head affectionately.

"Well, you're not. You're a patriot and a fearless warrior and that is exactly what we're going to need tonight if we are all to get out alive."

29

"WE can't leave without Godrig," said Boudica resolutely.

"Agreed," said Bodvoc, "but I've also got to find out as much as I can about Cartimandua's plans. It could be critical to the success of Caradoc's rebellion."

"I'll take you to her quarters."

Boudica, Chiomara and the druid were standing on the straw-strewn floor of the barn. The moon was high in the sky and it was close to midnight.

As they hurried through the sleeping town, Chiomara couldn't help asking Boudica, "Have you really met King Caradoc?"

Briefly Boudica explained how and then said, "But, Bodvoc, how did you know about that?"

"Prasutagus told me."

"Oh, I thought his visits to Camulodunon were secret."

"They were. Only Caradoc and I knew about them. He told me about finding you at Camulodunon the day I brought your father's body back..."

"You brought him back?" interrupted Boudica.

"Yes," said Bodvoc. "As I told you, druids can travel where others can't. It wouldn't have been safe for Prasutagus to do it."

"But what if you'd been caught by the Romans?"

"I wasn't."

Boudica's mind was reeling. Not only had she completely misjudged Bodvoc, but she was greatly in his debt for without him she could not have set her father's spirit free.

"I didn't realize. How can I thank you?"

Bodvoc shook his head.

"There's no need. A great injustice was done to Jodoc. Bringing him home was the least I could do."

Silently the three of them crept past the barns and silos and towards the pens where the Brigantes kept their herds. The sheep and pigs were sleepy. A cow let out a docile moo as they passed but it was not enough to disturb anyone.

Ahead of them was the meeting hall and temple which they skirted round to the quarter where the Brigantian homes were. By now most of them were dark but, as Boudica had hoped, one fire was still burning brightly. Cartimandua would be drinking for many more hours.

"That's it," she whispered to Bodvoc, pointing to the largest house round which the other smaller buildings clustered.

"Right, I'll see what I can find out," whispered Bodvoc. "You find Prince Godrig. We'll meet by the gap in the wall no later than when the moon touches that branch."

Boudica calculated how much time she had left; it would be enough if everything went smoothly.

"Where's your horse?" she asked.

Bodvoc described a dip in the forest. It was only just beyond the clearing where they'd left Kelpa and Cerrig.

"Good luck," said Bodvoc as he hurried off.

"Which way do we go?" asked Chiomara.

Boudica presumed Godrig would be in her old quarters, sharing with Hendra and Argent.

"Over here."

They crept to a low thatched building.

"Wait outside and keep a look out. Hoot twice if there's any trouble."

Cautiously Boudica lifted the fur that hung across the doorway. Inside she could see embers glowing dully in the hearth. Her heart began to pound. If Hendra woke up she'd scream and in no time the whole town would be upon them. She must be as silent as a deer. She crept into the dark room. *Wait*, she told herself, listening to the heavy breathing of the sleeping women, *give your eyes time to adjust*. Now she could see the outline of Hendra's ample tummy. She was lying flat on her back, lost to the world. Boudica glanced to the left to where Argent slept. She was there too. Godrig should be on the far side of the hut.

She shuffled forward slowly to the area furthest from the fire, where she used to sleep. Then she knelt down. Godrig's fur must be here. She felt something soft and patted it gently, not wanting to shock him too much, but there was no one there. She felt frantically to the right and left but the bearskin was empty.

Boudica knelt back, racking her brains for where else in the hut he might sleep. The space wasn't large and Hendra and Argent used all of it efficiently. Godrig must be sleeping somewhere else, but where? She couldn't possibly search every hut and not get caught.

And then, as if things weren't bad enough, she heard, "Whoo, whoo!"

It was Chiomara warning her. But the hoot was high-pitched and strangled, as if Chiomara was struggling to get her breath. Her friend was telling her they were in trouble and it sounded serious.

30

BOUDICA turned round as the pelt that covered the doorway was pulled aside and in the moonlight she saw Chiomara slip in. She crept across the hut as fast as she dared.

"What is it?" Boudica whispered.

"Bodvoc's been caught. I saw him marched away by four guards."

"Are you sure it was him?"

"Of course I am. He was shouting 'How dare you treat a druid like this?' and cursing them for putting their hands on him."

"Where did they take him?"

"I don't know; towards the palace. Where's Prince Godrig?"

"Not here," answered Boudica grimly.

She could sense that Chiomara was as worried as she was – the Brigantes might suspect Bodvoc was not alone They had to be careful; the slightest mistake could be fatal. Just then Hendra sighed and heaved herself over onto her side. The girls froze, but the loud snores continued.

"Would she help us?" whispered Chiomara.

Boudica thought for a moment. Hendra had been

good to her during her year with the Brigantes. She'd looked after her and had covered for her whenever she could to keep her out of trouble with Queen Cartimandua. But her first loyalty would always be to her tribe. If Boudica forced her to choose between them she would choose the Brigantes.

"No," she said quietly.

"Is there anybody else?" Chiomara sounded desperate. "Otherwise how are we going to find out where Prince Godrig is?"

Boudica was about to shake her head when the image of red-headed Culann came into her mind. The Brigantes had given him a home, for sure, but they would never make him a warrior. Although he'd grown up with them, he'd always been treated as an outsider. Culann had a strong sense of right and wrong and would be appalled by the queen's treachery. If anyone would help them it was him.

Boudica hugged Chiomara, her emerald eyes flashing with excitement.

"You're so clever! There is one person. Come on."

Boudica led the way to Culann's home which was set apart from the others as a protection against fire. He slept in the back of the forge in an area separated off by a thick tartan blanket. She put her ear to the door and heard a low growl.

"Mutta, it's Boudica. Don't you know me?"

There was an excited bark and the thump of a wagging tail. Boudica went in with Chiomara following close behind.

"Who's there?" said a voice.

Culann stood in the moonlight wearing only britches with a dagger in his hand. His tense, freckled face broke into a smile.

"Boudica, what on earth are you doing here?"

As fast as she could, Boudica explained the situation.

"If he's a prisoner," said Culann incredulously, "he doesn't know it. Queen Cartimandua told him his return has been delayed due to the Roman invasion, but he would be collected as soon as King Prasutagus could arrange it."

"That's not the only problem," said Boudica and she told him about Bodvoc.

"So, you see," she concluded, "we need your help. We can't find Prince Godrig and they've got Druid Bodvoc. Will you do it, Culann?"

There was a heavy silence. Boudica watched Culann's face intently. If he refused she didn't know what they would do next.

"If I do, I can never return to the tribe," said Culann slowly. "Even if they don't find out, I'd always be hiding something from them and that's not my way."

Boudica was crestfallen. Of course he couldn't betray his tribe. She never would.

"I understand," she said. "Just give us time to get

away. You'll do that for us, won't you?"

"I haven't finished yet," said Culann. "I will help you and then I'll leave Canna and find my real tribe, the one that I got separated from all those years ago."

"Really?" said Boudica, so relieved she could have hugged him.

"Yes. I can't live under the rule of a queen who'd do a deal with the Romans. Now, come on. I know where Prince Godrig is and I think I know how to get him out."

31

CULANN slipped behind the tartan curtain and emerged wearing plaid trousers, a brown wool shirt and a warm cape. He threw a bundle of clothing onto a blanket and then collected a hammer, tongs and a long, hooked metal stick from the forge.

"I can't take the anvil, but I'll need these to get work while I search for my tribe," he explained.

"How will you know if you've found them?" asked Boudica.

"I hope I'll just sense that I'm home," said Culann simply.

Boudica understood exactly what he meant. Chiomara and Belos could not have been more welcoming, but their home was not hers.

Culann took one last lingering look at the forge. As soon as they were outside he flung his bag over the high fence. It landed with a heavy thud.

"I'll collect it later, when we're on our way."

"So, where is Prince Godrig?" Boudica asked as they tiptoed through the dark, away from the forge.

"As he's a prince, Queen Cartimandua found him space in the royal quarters. He's been quite ill. I think it's the cold that's got to him. In the end Hendra insisted he spend a month in bed and he does seem to be a bit better for it."

"Oh," said Boudica. This was going to be harder than she'd thought. "Can we get him out tonight?"

"I think so," said Culann. "No one will stop me going to his room as I spent a lot of time with him when he was sick."

"But it's so late," interrupted Chiomara. "If anyone sees you, won't they be suspicious?"

"It'll be fine. I've lived in Canna for twelve years and everyone trusts me. Wait there." Culann pointed to a derelict round house whose thatch had half fallen in. "I won't be long."

I hope you're right, thought Boudica as he disappeared into the night.

In no time Culann was back leading Godrig by the hand. Boudica was shocked by how fragile the young boy looked. His little face was thin and pale and his skin was waxy but the thing that concerned her most was the feverish look in his eyes.

"Are you all right?" she asked.

"Yes, just a little hot," he answered. "Culann's told me what's going on."

"We must leave now," said Chiomara. "It's not long till daybreak."

"But we must get Bodvoc first," said Boudica.

Chiomara shook her head.

"Boudica, be reasonable," she said. "Right now we can

save the prince as King Prasutagus wanted us to. Bodvoc is a grown-up. He can look after himself."

"If we leave him, Queen Cartimandua will kill him before the day is out," said Boudica stubbornly. "He tried to save my father; I can't just leave. Don't you see that?"

"But rescuing Prince Godrig means King Prasutagus can join the rebellion," said Chiomara, looking exasperated. "It's what we came for. It's the most important thing."

Chiomara didn't understand. Boudica had completely misjudged Bodvoc and this might be her only chance to make amends. But Chiomara was right about Godrig – they had to get the prince out of Canna as soon as possible.

"You don't need *me* to rescue Godrig," said Boudica. "Take him to the place where we left the horses and if I'm not there by dawn, make sure that he gets back safely. You know the way home."

"I can't go without you," protested Chiomara.

"You have to," said Boudica. "He's far too young to get home alone. We have to separate. It's the only way."

It wasn't just Godrig's age that was troubling her, but his health. He wasn't well enough to handle a horse alone. If they were lucky, he would just about manage to cling onto one of them on the journey home.

"But how can you free Bodvoc by yourself?" pleaded Chiomara. "You don't stand a chance."

"She won't be alone," said Culann, who had not said a

word since spiriting Prince Godrig from the palace. "I'm going too."

32

BOUDICA and Culann accompanied Godrig and Chiomara to the gap in the fence.

"Good luck," said Chiomara. "We'll wait until sunrise."

"But not a moment longer," said Boudica. "Promise me that. You must get the prince home."

Chiomara nodded solemnly. Then she slipped through the hole and out of Canna.

"Do you have a weapon?" asked Godrig.

Boudica shook her head. The only thing she was carrying was a pocket knife that she used for cutting up fruit.

"Then take this."

Godrig pulled back his cape to reveal a silver sword hanging from a belt round his waist. He undid the buckle. "It's no use to me."

The sword looked ridiculously large for him, Boudica thought, taking the weapon. He must barely be able to lift it.

"What next?" asked Culann once Godrig had disappeared through the hole.

"Do you have any idea where Bodvoc is?"

"In a grain pit. That's where prisoners are always held."

"Let's go then."

They walked back past the palace and Hendra and Argent's house to the other side of town, taking care to stay in the shadows at all times.

"There," whispered Culann as they turned the last corner.

Less than twenty yards away four hefty men were crouching round a small fire, warming their hands, talking and sharing a bottle of mead. Beyond them, six large, wicker squares, like rugs woven awkwardly from sticks, lay on the ground in a grid-like pattern. They were the lids of the grain pits where the Brigantes stored wheat and corn over the winter. One pit was always empty and whichever it was, was now a temporary prison.

Boudica looked gloomily at the pits and then at the Brigantian warriors. The fire was burning brightly and there was nowhere to hide, just an open space and beyond that the town walls. They would be seen as soon as they came out from behind the hut where they were sheltering.

Suddenly the men laughed raucously and one of them leant over and thumped the lid of the nearest pit.

"Stop whinging!" he ordered. "Queen Cartimandua will sort you out soon enough."

Although they now knew where Bodvoc was, if anything it made things worse. He couldn't have been closer to his guards.

"We'd be mad to try and get him out," said Culann.

"Let's wait and see if they move him. We might have more of a chance later."

"No," said Boudica. "The queen will kill him as soon as she finds Godrig gone. She'll want to make an example of him in front of the whole tribe."

A straightforward rescue was hopeless but there had to be another way. Boudica wracked her brains.

"Could someone else help us? What about that king, Caradoc, you talked about? Is he here?" asked Culann.

"Not as far as I know."

Boudica glanced at the sky. Already it had lost a little of its darkness and the stars were shining less brightly. The night was nearly over. They had an hour at most. They had to do something, now. Suddenly she had an idea: it was rash and it might very well not work, but it was better than sitting here, waiting to be caught by the Brigantes.

"There is one person we could use," she said, her eyes flashing mischievously.

"Who?"

"Princess Bridgette."

"What are you talking about? You should've heard the things she said about the Iceni once you'd all left Canna. She'd never help you."

"Then we'll have to make her, won't we? Come on."

Boudica crouched behind a wicker basket of rotting vegetables. The smell was dreadful but it was perfectly positioned just opposite the royal enclosure. From there she had an excellent view of Culann disappearing once more into the palace. One of the guards at the entrance gave him a cheery wave as he approached.

"Who's the queen sent for now?"

"Princess Bridgette. She wants her to meet someone."

"Bit late for that, isn't it?"

Culann shrugged nonchalantly. "Tell that to the queen!" he joked as he was waved on his way.

A minute later he emerged with Bridgette dressed only in a white linen shift with a fur round her shoulders. Her black hair was dishevelled and she was yawning widely.

"Are you quite sure Mother wants me now?" she said petulantly. "If you're wrong, I'll be furious."

"Those are my orders and we must hurry up. We don't want to keep the queen hanging around."

Boudica crept behind the corner of the nearest house and waited, ready to pounce. Her timing had to be perfect. Bridgette must have no time to cry out or fight back. It would help that she was sleepy and it was dark.

"Goodness, I'm freezing," moaned Bridgette as she turned the corner. "This had better be important."

Boudica leapt out and pulled a piece of cloth ripped from her skirt tight round the princess's mouth, gagging her. At the same time Culann grabbed Bridgette's hands and tied them securely behind her back with a rope. The princess was so shocked she had no time to react, but as soon as she saw who her assailant was Bridgette's eyes blazed with fury. The last time she had seen her, Boudica was handing out food like a servant. Well, the tables were turned now.

"Calm down, Bridgette," said Boudica firmly. "You'll be with your mother soon enough, but first you're going to help me."

The princess made a muffled protest and kicked out. Boudica unsheathed Godrig's sword and held it up.

"It's sharp, so don't mess around, or I'm warning you, I'll use it."

She pushed Bridgette in front of her, pressing the tip of the sword into the princess's back, so that she could feel it through her fur.

"Culann, go to the paddock and drive the Brigantes' horses away into the forest – that'll stop them chasing after us once we're out of here – then tie Kelpa up by that oak tree next to the gates and go and join Chiomara."

"What are you talking about?" said Culann. "I'm staying with you."

"You've already done enough," said Boudica, "and anyway I need you to get Kelpa. I'm the one who's got business with the queen."

33

QUICKLY Boudica marched the squirming princess through Canna, with one hand on her shoulder and the other on Godrig's sword.

Two guards stood at the entrance to the banqueting hall, each holding a spear. As soon as the girls came in sight one of them called out, "Oi, what's going on? Stop there!"

"I'm going to untie your gag," Boudica whispered into Bridgette's ear, "and you are going to do *exactly* as I say. Do you understand?"

She pushed the sword just a little harder to remind Bridgette of its lethal presence.

The princess nodded frantically. She was trembling all over. *Good*, thought Boudica, *I need you to be terrified.*

"Order them to put their spears down and go and get your mother. Now."

A moment later, Queen Cartimandua came striding out of the roundhouse, quivering with rage.

"What on earth are you doing, Boudica? Let my daughter go this instant or I'll have you killed."

Don't even flinch, Boudica told herself over and over again. She met the queen's gaze and then pulled Bridgette closer to her and the sword. The princess whimpered pathetically.

"Mother, she's hurting me."

"How dare you?" said the queen. "Are you mad? You're a disgrace to your tribe!"

"Me?" said Boudica, her voice resolute and calm. "Me? How can you criticize me after what you've done?"

"What are you talking about?"

"Your friends – the Romans. They murdered my father and yet you're stopping us from taking revenge. Where's your loyalty? It's not me that's the disgrace, it's you."

"You don't know what you're talking about," said the queen, taking a step forward.

"If you come any closer, I'll kill Bridgette. I swear I will."

The queen stopped and stared at the wild-eyed girl. There was something chilling about her tone and the intensity of those eyes, but she was only a child. The situation was ridiculous.

"You don't have it in you," taunted the queen. "You don't have the guts."

Boudica pressed the sword a little harder. She didn't want to injure Bridgette, not because she didn't dare, but because it didn't suit her plan. It was a battle of wills between her and Cartimandua and she had to win.

"Mother, for the gods' sake, give her whatever she wants," Bridgette cried out piteously.

The queen paused.

"Well, Boudica, what *do* you want?" she asked. "Prince

Godrig, I suppose?"

"No," said Boudica. "I have him already."

Queen Cartimandua couldn't hide her astonishment. Boudica was triumphant. The more surprising and invincible she appeared to be, the more likely it was that the queen would do her bidding.

"I want Bodvoc," she said.

"Bodvoc?" Without taking her eyes off Boudica and her daughter, the queen called out sharply, "Guards, bring the druid to us now."

They waited for what felt like an age. The sky was now distinctly grey. Chiomara should be leaving soon.

Bridgette whimpered again. The girl seemed to have no pride. *If I were ever in this situation*, Boudica thought, *I'd have more self-respect.* Still that pathetic sound was the one thing that was keeping Boudica safe from Cartimandua's wrath.

"Here he is," said Cartimandua at last, holding out one end of a rope. The other end was tied around the druid's wrists. "My daughter for Bodvoc."

She spoke as if she were trying to reason with a truculent child.

"Do you really think I'm that stupid?" said Boudica. "You can have Bridgette when we're outside the gates."

"Mother, don't let her, take me. Stop her please," sobbed the princess.

"If you want your daughter alive, do as I say. Have your men open the gates."

A vein was throbbing in Cartimandua's neck, but she shoved the druid forward.

"Men, do as she asks."

"And then get them to come back here," commanded Boudica. "I don't want anyone following me."

"I will," said the queen, "but I'm warning you, if Bridgette is out of my sight, even for a moment, I'll tell my men to kill the lot of you. I won't have my daughter taken hostage by you or anyone else. Do you understand?"

Boudica knew that Cartimandua wasn't bluffing now. She began walking backwards across the square with Bodvoc on her right and the whimpering princess on her left.

"Walk slowly and calmly," she instructed Bodvoc quietly under her breath. "Don't run. I've got a horse waiting just outside the gates."

The queen and the Brigantian warriors stayed absolutely still and watched as they backed away.

"I don't believe it," murmured Bodvoc, loosening the rope round his wrist.

They continued pacing steadily backwards across the square, towards the gates. Beyond them lay open land. They were moments away from freedom.

"Keep moving, Bridgette," ordered Boudica as they backed over the drawbridge. The queen was staring after them, daring Boudica to let her daughter drop out of sight.

"Kelpa should be on our left."

She glanced towards the oak tree but there was no horse. What was going on? Had Culann mistaken the tree and tied the stallion somewhere else? She looked frantically round, but there was no horse anywhere.

"What's wrong?" asked Bodvoc.

"I don't know," said Boudica, bewildered. "It should be here."

Two hundred yards away the Brigantes were frozen but they wouldn't stay still for long.

"We're going to have to run for it," said Boudica.

"What? We won't even reach the forest. They've got chariots and spears."

"But they haven't got horses. Look, the pasture's empty."

"Great," said Bodvoc heavily.

"Have you got any better ideas? We'll back off as far as we can, then dump Bridgette and run for the trees. Hopefully we'll catch one of their horses. We've got a head start. Let's go!"

Boudica pushed Bridgette to the ground, shoved the sword back in its scabbard and ran. She could hear Bodvoc panting right behind her. The woods were less than a hundred yards away, now fifty, now they were in, slashing their way through the brambles and bracken.

"Down the hill!" shouted Boudica. "There's a stream at the bottom. One of their horses might be there."

Their chances of escape were impossibly slim, but what else could they do? Behind her, in the distance, she could hear screams – the Brigantes were on the move.

"Come on!"

She grabbed Bodvoc by the hand and pulled him along.

Something white flashed past them in the clearing ahead and a high-pitched howl brought them skidding to a halt. They had run straight into a pack of wolves. They were bunched together, growling horribly and baring their long white teeth. Their yellow eyes glowed menacingly in the early morning light.

"Quick! We must go the other way." said Bodvoc.

But the ferocious din of Cartimandua's men was getting closer and closer.

"We can't," said Boudica. "It's hopeless. We're trapped."

34

THEY stood frozen in the wood. Boudica pulled out Godrig's sword but it was a hopeless gesture. In front of them was a pack of snarling wolves, behind them the Brigantes marauding through the forest.

A spear screeched through the air, bouncing off a tree just yards away from them. Boudica looked at Bodvoc.

"I'm sorry. You would have been better off without me."

"Don't be stupid," he said. "You did your best."

But suddenly, as they waited to see who got them first, a black horse with a red-haired boy on its back came thundering through the forest, scattering the wolves. It was Culann on Kelpa.

"Get up!" he shouted.

As they scrambled onto the stallion another spear screamed through the trees. A huge man ran into the clearing, whirling an axe round his head, but he was too late; Kelpa was galloping off up the valley.

"Sorry I wasn't there," shouted Culann over his shoulder once they were safely away. "I forgot about Probas. He guards those horses as if they're his own children. By the time I'd sorted him out you were already out of the gates."

"It doesn't matter," said Boudica, smiling at last. "We're safe now."

They reached Chiomara just as the first rays of sunlight shone through the trees. She was already on Cerrig with Prince Godrig behind her, wrapped up in a fur. In her hand she held the reins of a grey mare and the bundle that Culann had thrown over the wall.

"Thank goodness!" she said when they arrived. "I was just about to give up on you."

Bodvoc slid off Kelpa's rump. "Thank you for getting my horse."

"Right, are we ready to go?" said Boudica. "Culann, what are you doing?"

Culann had jumped off Kelpa as well.

"I'm not coming with you," he said, taking his bundle. "I'm going north to find the Caledonii. Hendra once told me she thought I was one of them."

"But their lands are days away," protested Boudica. "Queen Cartimandua will catch you before you get near them."

"She's not after me. It's you she wants."

"But you've no horse, nothing. And what if they won't accept you? You could be tribeless – do you realize what that means? You'll be shunned by everyone you meet."

"I know that," said Culann.

"So, come and live with the Iceni for a winter. You'll

be a hero. If you still want to go, you can leave in the spring when the journey will be easier."

Culann shook his head doggedly.

"I've waited a long time to make this journey. Now I've started I can't stop. Like you, I just want to go home."

Boudica didn't try and dissuade him further. She understood his need to find his own people and perhaps even the mother who'd been dragged screaming from her baby when the camp was raided.

"Well, at least take Kelpa," she said impulsively.

"I can't do that. He belonged to your father."

"It's what he would have wanted. Without you we wouldn't have got out of Canna alive. You'll make much better time with Kelpa – you might even reach the Caledonian lands before the snows come."

"But how will you manage?" asked Culann.

"There are four of us and two mares. We'll be fine."

"But we must get going," said Chiomara.

Culann patted Kelpa's nose. "I'll look after him, I promise."

Boudica climbed up behind Bodvoc and they set off at a gallop, Culann heading north and the rest of them south. She looked back at the red-haired boy as he disappeared between the trees. He was a Caledonian, she was an Icenian, but they had worked well together. If only the tribes of Britain would do the same.

35

THE sky was grey and misty when they arrived at the river beyond the ridge above Canna. The only thing Boudica had to sacrifice to Andraste was Godrig's sword. Quickly she broke the blade on a rock, as she had seen her father do, thanked the goddess for her help so far and begged for her blessing on the final part of their journey.

They rode all day, stopping only once to water the horses. Boudica was so hungry her stomach ached but they had to keep going because they would not be safe until they reached the strange wooden statue that marked the border between Brigantian and Corieltauvian lands.

Evening came and still they travelled on. Surely it couldn't be far now. The moors were behind them and they were riding through pine forests. At every bend in the track Boudica prayed to see the carved ghoulish face.

Bodvoc shouted something but it was impossible to hear over the pounding hooves. He slowed down.

"What is it?"

"Look ahead," said the druid. "Don't you see them?"

In the dusk, Boudica could just make out a party of

men on horseback thundering towards them. Had the Brigantes rounded up their horses, taken a different route and got ahead of them? She swallowed hard. The bridle path was hedged in by dense trees. There was nowhere to take cover and no point in trying to outride anyone; their horses were exhausted.

"Why are we slowing down?" asked Prince Godrig, peeping out from his warm fur.

"Someone's coming. It could be Cartimandua's men," said Chiomara quietly.

Nervously, they watched the approaching horses. There were eight riders led by a short, wiry man with fair hair.

"They aren't Brigantes," said Bodvoc suddenly. "It's Caradoc," and he spurred his horse forward to meet the rebel king. "So, you got my message?"

"Yes, but I was way over in the west so it took a while to reach me," said Caradoc. "We were on our way to help you, but I see you've done perfectly well without us. Come, the border's just this way."

Caradoc led them along the bridle path, past the hideous wooden statue and into more trees.

"We'll camp here for the night," he said. "The Brigantes will never find us."

Boudica had a hundred questions to ask but first she helped Chiomara get Prince Godrig off Cerrig and took him to a warm place by the fire.

One of Caradoc's men was roasting wood pigeon.

"Do you think you can you eat anything?" Boudica asked Godrig gently.

"I think so," said the prince. "I'm tired but I feel better now we're away from that place."

Boudica pressed her hand against his forehead. It was warmer than hers, but not alarmingly so.

She brought him some food.

"Go and join King Caradoc – he wants to talk to you," said Chiomara. "I'll stay with the prince."

Boudica sat down next to the king.

"You wanted me, sir."

"Yes. I want to congratulate you. Bodvoc has told me everything. You've done well. The Iceni should be very proud."

Boudica didn't know what to say but she blushed with pleasure. She hoped the rebel king knew how much his praise meant to her.

"So can the rebellion start now?" she asked, after a pause.

"Not quite yet. There are some last tribes that need convincing but it won't be too long. Stories of Roman cruelty spread further and further each day. Tell King Prasutagus he'll hear from me soon and that, thanks to you, he'll be free to join us."

"Won't you tell him yourself, sir? It might help." Boudica was a little apprehensive of the reception she might receive from Prasutagus when she got back to Sinovix. After all she had gone against his orders.

"No, I have work to do in the north: we must catch Agron if he hasn't been finished off by Cartimandua already. I'll be leaving very early in the morning. Don't worry about Prasutagus, I'm sure he'll be very proud of you."

"Thank you. Good luck, sir," said Boudica as she went to rejoin Chiomara and Godrig.

"We'll need it," said the rebel king. "But remember, if we don't succeed this time, we'll try and try again. One day the Romans will be driven from this land. It doesn't belong to them, and our people will not consent to be their slaves for ever."

36

WHEN Bodvoc, Godrig, Chiomara and Boudica rode into Sinovix, it seemed every single member of the tribe was waiting to greet them. Boudica couldn't believe the welcome they received and how quickly the story of their adventures was passed around.

Even King Prasutagus seemed delighted. He raised his hands for silence.

"Tonight we will hold a feast in honour of the safe return of my brother, Chiomara and Bodvoc, but in particular of Boudica. She had the courage to do what no man here has done. She liberated a prince from under the noses of the Brigantes." Boudica beamed with pride. "Until tonight the weary travellers will rest."

Without thinking, Boudica walked with Chiomara towards the town gates but before she had got very far Tessa ran up and held her in her arms.

"Don't go that way. Mother wants you to come home. Since King Prasutagus told her where you'd gone she's been so worried about you. She begs for your forgiveness."

"Go on," said Chiomara. "It's time."

Dagma was waiting by the door, tense and anxious.

"I've lit a fire and there's food waiting for you.

Perhaps Chiomara would like to join us. From now on she'll always be welcome."

"Thank you," said Boudica, "but she wants to be with her father now."

Dagma bit her lip, trying to control her emotions.

"Boudica, King Prasutagus came to talk to me the day you left. He guessed what you were up to and thought I should know. He also told me about the death of your father and how you made sure he was buried properly. I felt then that the way I've treated you these past months is unforgivable. When I heard what you had gone to do … it brought me to my senses."

Boudica didn't want her mother to say any more. They had both been as stubborn as each other, but it was behind them now.

"It was my fault too," said Boudica. "I feel terrible about what happened to father."

"But I shouldn't have blamed you for telling the truth about that dagger. What choice did you have?" said Dagma, hugging her tightly and wiping the tears from her eyes. "Now, please come in. I've made you your favourite porridge."

Boudica ate, then she flopped on the bearskin and fell asleep in her clothes. It was the first time she had slept in comfort for ten days.

Later that evening Dagma had to shake Boudica hard to wake her.

"I can't let you sleep any longer. You can't be late for the feast in your honour."

Her mother had already laid out a clean woollen skirt of red and blue tartan, a matching shawl, and a linen shirt.

Boudica sat up. It was strange being back in her home after all this time. She washed her face and hands in a bowl of cold water.

"Come on," said Dagma. "People have been pouring into the town all afternoon."

Boudica got dressed as quickly as she could and then allowed her mother to brush her hair.

"King Prasutagus holds you in very high regard, you know," said Dagma as she combed the tangles out.

"Mother, what are you talking about?" said Boudica.

"I'm telling you, he sang your praises the night he came to see me. It can't be long before he starts looking for a wife. Perhaps he'll cast an eye in your direction."

Boudica stared at her mother. She was impossible. The family honour had only just been restored and she was scheming already.

"Please don't start that again," said Boudica, shaking her head. "I'm far too young to marry. Find Tessa a husband before you even think about me."

Tessa and Dagma went with her to the feast. The sun had set and the market square was illuminated with flares. King Prasutagus was standing at the entrance to the hall. His hair was spiked with chalk and he was wearing his brightest cape.

"I was beginning to think you weren't coming," he said holding out his arm to lead her in.

The hall was full of people. Chiomara, Prince Godrig, Belos, and all the people of Sinovix were there and many other Iceni from the outlying villages. Everyone was smiling at her and cheering; the noise was overwhelming.

"Come this way," said the king and led her towards the stone circle in the centre of the hall where the Icenian warriors were seated. As they approached the entrance, Boudica let go of his arm.

"I can't go in there," she whispered.

"Yes, you can," said the king. "You've earned the right to be an Icenian warrior. There is no other place for you."

Boudica didn't know what to say. She hadn't expected this at all. "But I don't have a shield."

"Bodvoc can help," said the king.

The druid was standing at the entrance to the circle. He turned round and pulled out a bronze shield decorated with red coloured glass in the circular patterns Jodoc always had engraved on his armour. It glowed in the firelight creating shimmering reflections on the ceiling.

Boudica stared at it.

"It's just like my father's old shield," she said at last.

"It *is* his shield," said Prasutagus, "and I only wish he were here to see you use it."

Bodvoc held it out. It was heavier than she expected but once she had her hand through the sling she realized how perfectly weighted it was. It was not only a thing of beauty but a weapon fit for war.

"Now take your proper place," said the king.

As if in a dream Boudica walked into the magical circle and propped her shield against the wall, like the other Icenian warriors. A cheer ricocheted around the hall. Not only the king, but all the Iceni, accepted her as a warrior.

As she sat down she silently said a prayer to the goddess Andraste: *Please make me worthy of this honour*.

King Prasutagus came and placed his shield next to hers.

"If Jodoc could see you now, he would be very proud of you. Like him, you are a true warrior of the Iceni."

The End

WHAT HAPPENED NEXT

IN about AD46, when she was roughly sixteen years old Boudica married Prasutagus, king of the Iceni. The Romans now had complete control of the south of England but they allowed some client kings, like Prasutagus, to rule their ancient kingdoms.

In AD47 the Iceni led an attack against Rome. Some neighbouring tribes joined in the revolt, but not enough for it to succeed against the might of Rome. Prasutagus was allowed to keep his throne but only on condition that the Iceni paid the Romans punishing taxes.

Queen Cartimandua of the Brigantes did not participate in the rebellion and it appears some of her tribe were unhappy about this, for at around this time there was an outbreak of violence in Brigantian territory. Cartimandua only managed to keep her throne by appealing to the Romans for support. They executed the Brigantian ringleaders as an example to Britons of what would happen if they did not do Rome's bidding.

Caradoc continued to try and persuade the tribes of Britain to unite and fight. In AD52 he joined with the Silures of southern Wales and led his men into a decisive battle against the Twentieth Legion, the legion that had been stationed at Camulodunon, now called Colchester, just south of Icenian territory. Although Caradoc was defeated, he and his band of rebels inflicted heavy casualties on the Romans – it is estimated that over a thousand were killed in one day. Having come so close to success, Caradoc was convinced the Britons could defeat Rome. He went in disguise to the Brigantes, to try and persuade them to rise up against their queen and help, but he underestimated the cunning of Queen Cartimandua who captured him and promptly handed him over to the Roman Governor. Caradoc was taken in chains to Rome where he was tried for treason before the Senate. He is recorded as saying: "Can you, then, who have got so many possessions, covet our poor huts? ... If you Romans choose to lord it over the world, does that mean that we have to accept slavery?" His defence of the rebellion was so noble that the Senators decided to pardon him and he lived out the rest of his days as a celebrity in Rome.

Meanwhile the Romans were unhappy with their latest conquest. They thought Britain would be rich in minerals but most of what they found was of poor quality. Disappointed, they began to plunder. They captured many Britons and sent them overseas to serve as slaves in the Roman Empire. They confiscated land to give to retiring legionaries, driving out the original owners or forcing them to work for the new landlord. Dissenters had their heads left on spikes as a warning to others. All this caused even more resentment among the Britons and the druids played a vital role in spreading this discontent. Their religious and spiritual status meant they could move freely from one tribe to another, and slowly they began to spread the message that something had to be done.

The Iceni escaped the worst of the Roman atrocities, but in AD61 at the age of forty King Prasutagus suddenly died, probably in a hunting accident. In his will he left half his kingdom to Rome and the other half to his two daughters. Boudica, his wife, was to rule as queen until the girls, aged around nine and eleven, came of age.

It is presumed that Prasutagus bequeathed half his goods to Rome in the belief that they would then allow his family and tribe some independence. If so, he was mistaken. Only days after the king's death, the Roman Governor ordered his men to enter the royal residence and seize all Icenian property.

We do not know whether Queen Boudica was happy with the agreement her husband had reached with the Romans after the failed uprising of AD47, but we do know that she was incensed by the Governor's instructions and vowed to stop all land, jewels and horses being stolen from her tribe. The Governor was furious. No Briton would be allowed to defy Rome, especially not a woman. He would humiliate her and show the Iceni who was now their ruler.

Early one morning, legionaries rode into Boudica's

town and ambushed the queen. She and her two young daughters were forced to strip naked and beaten in front of the tribe.

Boudica was outraged and, once the Romans had left, challenged her people to avenge this terrible insult to their queen. She is said to have used a running hare to convince the Iceni to rally to her. The neighbouring tribe, the Trinovantes, who had borne the brunt of the Roman invasion, quickly decided to join her too. Many other tribes, though not the Brigantes, decided that they had also had enough. A rebellion was born.

South of the Icenian border, the town of Camulodunon was the administrative centre of Roman Britain and its largest military base. Led by the warrior queen, a huge army surrounded and attacked the town. The Romans took refuge in their temple. For two days the Britons laid siege to the building then Boudica ordered it to be destroyed. Brushwood was piled up round it and the temple was set alight killing many men, women and children. Boudica is said to have dedicated this sacrifice to the goddess of victory, Andraste.

Scenting triumph, she was determined to drive the Romans from Britain and avenge the wrongs they had done to her family. She destroyed their other towns – Londinium (now London), and Verulamium (St Albans). In these battles historians estimate that over 70,000 civilians were killed.

Boudica's army looked unstoppable as tribe after tribe joined the rebellion. But it was not. Paulinus, the most senior Roman soldier in Britain, was on a campaign in Wales to try and wipe out the druids on the Isle of Mona. When he received reports of Boudica's rebellion he immediately stopped his Welsh battles and, using the now well developed network of Roman roads, marched his men to the Midlands, determined to reassert Roman power.

Paulinus positioned his troops at the top of a valley with a wood behind him. On the morning of the battle Boudica gathered her warriors at the bottom. They must have been an awesome sight – over 100,000 Celts determined on revenge. Their faces would have been painted with blue paint and their hair spiked up with chalk. To show their fearlessness they wore little armour preferring instead just a sword and shield. The 13,000 Romans waiting for the charge at the top of the valley must have been terrified but they had some crucial advantages. They were trained soldiers, organized and disciplined.

Drunk with success from previous battles, the Britons were convinced victory was assured. Boudica drove a chariot among her soldiers with her two daughters sitting at the front. She reminded her army what they were fighting for – their freedom. In a rousing speech she promised this would be the decisive battle – she would either lead them to triumph or die.

So confident were the Britons, that a great crowd of women and children, travelling in wagons, camped at the bottom of the valley to watch the spectacle. This was to prove fatal.

Boudica gave the order for her army to attack. Her men charged, screaming and shouting, and were met by a shower of spears. Many were killed instantly. Warriors tripped over their fallen comrades but had no time to warn the men behind them to slow down. Into this confusion Paulinus sent the Roman cavalry. The Britons tried to retreat but were trapped by their own wagons, and the battle turned into a rout. It is believed 80,000 Britons were killed in one afternoon and, with them, all hopes of independence. Paulinus had quashed the rebellion and was a hero in Rome.

Boudica managed to escape in a chariot with her two young daughters. She knew that she would be shown no mercy by the Romans so she headed back to her ancestral tribal lands. Once in Icenian territory it is believed that she and her daughters went into a sacred oak forest and drank poison.

Boudica's death marked the end of the only rebellion to seriously threaten the Romans in Britain. Thereafter Rome sent many more soldiers to ensure that it could never happen again and they also did away with client states, including the Brigantes. Queen Cartimandua sought refuge from her own people with the Romans.

After the rebellion was defeated, the Romans studied

its causes. They realized that the mutiny had been sparked by their harsh treatment of the tribes, so a more just governor, Classicianus, was sent to rule Britain.

Under Classicianus, the benefits of the Roman Empire were gradually introduced to Britain. For the first time Britons experienced warm baths, underground heating and peace between warring tribes. In time the whole island, with the exception of Scotland, was brought under Roman rule.

Although Boudica herself was ultimately defeated by Rome, her story has lived on for over 2,000 years. She bravely challenged the most powerful empire the world had ever seen. She refused to give in against overwhelming odds and died fighting for her people's freedom, and so history remembers Boudica as the ultimate warrior queen.

AUTHOR'S NOTES

WHEN I first began to research the early years of Boudica's life I was surprised by how little historians know. There is no certainty about who her parents were, where she was born or how she came to be queen. In fact there is no mention of her in written history until the time of her famous rebellion.

When writing this story I have made sure that I have included the few facts that are recorded. The Romans did invade Britain during Boudica's childhood; she is likely to have come from a grand Icenian family and she would have spent time with a neighbouring tribe. I have also used the archaeological material available: Beltaine was an important Celtic festival; druids did wander between tribes and ferment rebellion; and hares were used to make important decisions.

The Iceni, Brigantes, Corieltauvi, Trinovantes, Caledonii, Silures and Atrebates are real British late Iron Age tribes. Queen Cartimandua, Caradoc, King Antedios and King Prasutagus are real people but, of course, I have had to imagine their characters. We do have some clues from the past. Queen Cartimandua did ally herself with the Romans at the expense of the southern tribes. Caradoc was a key figure in the rebellion. Prasutagus did take over from his father and then lead the Iceni to their first revolt. Finally, Boudica must have been a brave and daring warrior. Not only did she become one of the few Celtic queens but she led the only British rebellion in the history of the Roman Empire that came close to being successful.

Notes From the Past

CELTIC TRIBES: Two thousand years ago, at the time of the Roman Invasion, the people who lived in this country were called Britons. They spoke a language known as Celtic.

Britons were divided into many different tribes, each led by its own king or queen. These tribes often fought among themselves. This made it much easier for the Romans to invade and conquer all but modern day Scotland.

HOUSES: The Britons lived in small settlements of up to a couple of hundred people. They built round-houses from wood, mud and stone with thatched roofs. A central fire would heat the home and be used for cooking. A hole in the roof acted as a chimney, but the room would have been very smoky.

Villages were often built on hilltops with fences or ditches encircling them to make them easier to defend.

CLOTHES: Ancient Britons dressed in striped and checked clothes, similar to tartan. They were woven from wool and flax, and dyed using plants and minerals.

For special occasions, men spiked their hair with

lime and painted patterns on their arms and legs. Women wore cosmetics that they made themselves.

Jewellery was popular with both men and women.

METALWORK: Ancient Britons were skilled metal craftsmen. They worked with bronze, iron and gold. By the time Boudica was growing up, blacksmiths had perfected enamelling to produce beautiful colours. It was used on shields, swords, brooches, rings and torcs. Examples have been found by archaeologists in Celtic burial sites all over Britain.

EDUCATION: Children in ancient Britain did not attend formal school but learned from watching and helping their parents and other adults. It is thought that both boys and girls were taught to ride horses and fight using spears and swords.

Wealthy Britons sent their children to spend time with a neighbouring tribe. This forged links between tribes and helped reduce the incidence of wars.

FEASTING: When the Romans invaded they were amazed by the Britons' feasts. Whole tribes would gather to celebrate festivals or victories and consume vast quantities of food and drink. Alcohol was mainly ale and mead, brewed from honey, although by Boudica's time, southern tribes had begun to import wine from Europe. Meat, particularly pork and beef, roasted or boiled, was the main dish. The choicest cuts would be given to the bravest warriors.

RELIGION: The Britons were a superstitious people who worshiped many spirits and shrines. Their religion was closely tied to the natural world. They believed gods inhabited sacred places like forests and lakes as well as animals and plants. An oak tree overgrown with mistletoe was seen as especially magical. This is the origin of the tradition of kissing under mistletoe at Christmas.

In Boudica's time, Andraste, Goddess of Victory, was especially popular among the Iceni.

SACRIFICES: Britons made sacrifices to keep the gods happy. They threw precious weapons into lakes, rivers and bogs. In one site in Wales, archaeologists have found over 150 offerings including spears, swords and shields.

Britons also sacrificed animals and may have made human sacrifices as well. Tacitus, a Roman historian, reported that Boudica sacrificed many Romans to Andraste after the fall of Colchester, but his report may be unreliable as he was biased against the Britons.

DRUIDS: Ancient Britons held these men in high esteem as scholars, religious leaders, healers and seers. Druids were secretive, passing their wisdom from one generation to the next by memory, not by written texts. To qualify, a druid had to study for up to twenty years, learning by heart traditional stories, laws, spells and cures. The main centre of learning was on the Island of Anglesey in Wales, known as Mona. Druids travelled from all over Europe to study there.

FESTIVALS: Britons celebrated two main festivals: Samain and Beltaine. Samain marked the new year and was held around the end of October. It lives on in our Halloween. Beltaine, a festival marking the beginning of summer, took place in early May. Britons jumped fires, decorated their homes with spring flowers and danced. Maypole dancing is believed to have its origins in Beltaine.

HEADHUNTERS: The ancient Britons kept the heads of defeated enemies as trophies. They were placed in temples, nailed to doorways or even hung on warriors' saddles. The Britons believed that a person's head contained their soul, and by keeping the head they controlled the spirit.

BURIALS: Traditionally, ancient Britons were buried with the things they would need in the next life. Archaeologists have found graves containing chariots, weapons, jewellery and silver cups. Very few children's graves have been found. It is likely that, for some reason we don't yet understand, children didn't qualify for burial.

By the time of Boudica, funerals had changed. As a result of Roman influence from Gaul (modern day France), Britons began to burn their dead rather than bury them.